All at once he was back in the water off Repulse
Bay, and the water was red with blood, and there
were the strange popping sounds of the gun, and
the stench of blood and gasoline and the heat of
the flames, and unbearable pain. There were the
assassins. They would always be there, until he
killed them all, and then he would go home and
put the gun in a drawer and turn his attention to
other things, and killing would be something
other people did. But first, the job he had to do,
finding them and killing them, and nothing,
nothing, could sway him from that.

SCIMITAR

SCOTT STONE

SCIMITAR

WORLDWIDE ®

TORONTO • NEW YORK • LONDON • PARIS
AMSTERDAM • STOCKHOLM • HAMBURG
ATHENS • MILAN • TOKYO • SYDNEY

For my brother, Eb, in war and peace
a man of dignity and courage

SCIMITAR

A Worldwide Library Book/May 1989

ISBN 0-373-97102-8

A scimitar is a curved sword, probably of Persian origin but once used widely across the Middle East and with adaptations in Turkey and India. It is characterized generally by fine workmanship and a certain deadly grace. The sword was not designed for backhand use, nor for stabbing. Its sole function is to be a cutting weapon, and as such it has few peers.

ONE

OUT OF THE SEA the sun came like yellow fire, crackling along the surface and scattering heat and light. A wind that had sprung up before dawn died as suddenly as it had begun, and on the horizon the clouds began to flatten and disappear as the day came on, hot and glaring. Foliage near the shoreline began to lose its vivid green, and in the lee of the island the tide moved ponderously to push its salt-streaked edge onto the sand spit and disappear with a hissing sound, followed quickly by the hum of the water tumbling the round rocks of the beach as it made its way seaward again.

From the interior of the island came the sharp and sudden cry of a bird, and as if in echo there was the distant melancholy sound of a temple bell. The old fisherman heard the bell as he squatted and smoked and looked at the beach, where the tide was nudging a body higher up on the sand. There was a time, he thought, when I heard that bell clearly. Now it seems so soft. And once I could see for miles across the ocean; now I see . . . not so far. But I am alive and that one is not.

He studied the body, as he had since daylight.

A sailor from one of the passing freighters, perhaps. Big, and badly burned. As the body rolled naked in the surf he could see that parts of it were charred. One arm was bent at a strange angle. Perhaps, he thought, the compassionate Buddha had allowed him to die quickly, for such wounds would bring great pain. A *kwai-loh*, but with hair as dark as any Chinese.

The old fisherman threw his cigarette onto the sand and sat, considering. He had no intention of getting any closer to the body; the next high tide would be just before midday and could easily take the body back into the sea, where the sharks would consume it. He would not even mention it to the priests, for whom all life was sacred and all death to be celebrated, even the death of a *kwai-loh*. They would want to report the discovery of the body to the police. The old fisherman did not want to talk with anyone in authority. He hated all regulations and all who made them. He wanted only to fish, and to be left alone.

He settled the round straw hat closer over his eyes and peered at the body again. What the fire had not burned the sun would, and in no time at all, for the day was going to be hot. The sky looked like the inside of a pale rice bowl, cloudless and close and hard. The water held no whitecaps, and he knew there would be many fishing boats out today, but most of them would be on the windward side. The body was unlikely to be seen from any of the boats, and even if it were, those fishermen would probably ignore it, just as he would.

The old fisherman had spent his life on the island, leaving it only rarely and only for good reason. He remembered the few times he had taken a fishing boat north and east to Shek Kwu Chau and Cheung Chau, where he got the Hong Kong Yaumati Ferry to Peng Chau and on around the western point of Hong Kong to the Central District landing. It was a complicated trip during which he was crowded, jostled and hemmed in by buildings as well as people, and each time it was with a great sense of relief that he fled back to the island where he was born and where, with luck, he would live to a ripe old age and die some morning, peacefully, on the beach. But not like that one. That one was young and had suffered much and was dead long before he should have been. It came of being around too many people. People were dangerous. The old fisherman could say, quite honestly, that he had never had a close relationship with any other living human being—and he felt it a victory.

The tide was ebbing, and he picked up his pail and bamboo pole and straightened with a grunt, setting a course around the body for the place where he liked to sit and fish in the lee of the great gray-black rocks. He felt the heat of the sand under his bare feet, unusually hot for the hour but never too hot for him. He started to negotiate a wide arc around the body, to reach the rocks, but as he neared it he stopped to look in spite of himself. The *kwai-loh* was on his back, eyes open and staring.

As the fisherman looked at the eyes, one of them blinked.

The old man jumped as if he had touched fire. Then he stood still as stone, squinting at the body, his mind in confusion. It was not possible that this man could be alive. And yet... and yet, even as he watched, a grimace of pain crossed that foreign face, and this time both eyes focused on him in a look of pure desperation.

The *kwai-loh* lived, and now there would be trouble.

But he might not live long. The heat and the thirst would be bad enough for a healthy man, and this one was close to death. The old fisherman thought about it. He could walk on, around him to the rocks, and fish through the morning, and by the time he got back the *kwai-loh* would surely cease to be and the tide would take him away as if he were a piece of driftwood. Or he could, he thought, simply shove him into the sea now, taking no chances. He considered it.

As he stood there he again heard the small, melodic sound of the bell. If the priests found out what he had done there would be trouble. Better to tell the priests, perhaps. No, better to think about it some more. He turned to walk away and then glanced back, in time to see a look of anger in the man's eyes. Then the eyes closed.

He walked to the rocks and sat with the pail between his legs. In a few minutes he had secured the float and baited the hook and put the pail aside, settling down to face seaward, his back to the body. For a long time he sat there while the float bobbed in the eddies around the rocks and the bait dangled, untouched, beneath. He looked up at the sky and down at the float, then cursing his luck, he turned to look along the beach. The body was still there, rolling in the surge. And surely the man was dead by now.

The heat was building quickly and the sea had begun to glitter, with the angle of the sun striking the sets as the low waves slid shoreward. Time, he thought, to do one or the other. He retrieved his hook, losing the bait in the process, and was shortly following his own prints back to the vicinity of the body. He stared and finally shook his head. If the man were not dead now, he soon would be. No harm, he thought, in telling the priests. No hurry, either.

THE PAIN THAT HAD MADE him faint now lashed him awake, and he moaned in spite of himself. He was surprised, and not particularly pleased, to be alive. He was lying on some sort of pallet, and every place that his body touched felt like a flame licking him remorselessly. When he finally fell silent with a great effort of will, he tried to move his head, but it was heavy, heavy, and in a few moments he felt tears stinging his eyes. He stared straight up at the rough masonry above him, wondered briefly where he was and choked back another moan. The effort made him faint again. Later he woke briefly, badly needing water, and then fell asleep.

He might have slept minutes or days. The next time he stirred, the pain was still there, but he managed to fight back the sobs that he could feel building in him. The pain was universal; there wasn't an inch of him that escaped it. It erased all thought, all emotions; his mind was a red haze through which nothing would penetrate, ever again. When he was awake, however briefly, he wanted nothing more than to sleep again, but sleep was not a total relief from pain.

Once he awoke to find water dripping on his lips. He swallowed it mechanically. When he stirred again he was conscious of someone near him, but the idea took too much effort to pursue, and he simply closed his eyes and waited for whatever was coming—life, death, additional pain. It was a resignation that lasted a millisecond, for it was replaced by a thought that he later credited with saving his life. It came to him through the red haze, through the agony in his arm, through the total indignity of his position. It arced through his consciousness like a piece of flying steel, a metallic thought that forced his eyes open again and brought the semblance of a smile to lips that had cracked and peeled.

"CAN YOU HEAR ME?" the priest asked in English.

The man on the bed blinked his eyes.

"You must be in great pain. We are helping you, but you are badly burned."

The eyes blinked again.

"We must find out who you are, get you to a hospital."

This time there was no reaction. The eyes stared back at the priest, hard and unyielding.

FEELING HAD PRECEDED thought; pain came before feeling. At a time when he thought the pain was abating, or that he was so used to it that it became a part of his nature, the priests came back.

He felt, rather than saw them. Much of the time he lay with his eyes shut simply because it was less effort, but he was aware the priests had been around. He had no idea where he was or how long he had been there. He only knew, in the next few minutes, that they had propped him up and were rubbing something all over his body that felt like liquid fire. He groaned in spite of himself; the effort of half sitting, even with support, almost made him faint. The same priest who had spoken to him earlier leaned near his ear. "It is a balm. We use it to stop infections. We have rubbed this on you many times, while you were unconscious. It will hurt, but it will help. If you are hearing me, blink your eyes again, just once . . . Ah." The priest was smiling.

He brought him into focus with difficulty, but there was a definite smile that he could see. He also could see the robe, the shaved head, eyes that were wide, dark and glittering.

"Welcome back," the priest said.

He tried to form words, and failed. Instead he closed his eyes again while others were rubbing the salve into his burns. He must have fallen asleep that way, for when he opened his eyes again the men were gone and he was lying flat on the smooth pallet. The room was dark except for some light in a far corner. With enormous difficulty he raised his head slightly and saw a candle burning, and beyond it stone masonry. Even as he looked the candle wavered slightly in a breeze that came in through a high, narrow window to his left. He cut his eyes around to look through the window, but it was dark. He laid his head back and tried to think.

Memory came to him in a random fashion, like tracers arcing at him from different directions. Strongest were the flames, searing and spreading—he had been unable to get away from them. Then a face came back, the woman, turning to him and calling for help, only a second before her face flew apart in a red explosion. Vaguely he knew there was someone else there, someone he ought to think about, but his mind had shut down for the moment. The last thing he remembered before he fell asleep was the woman, in another time, when she had been laughing, her head back, her face animated and beautiful.

When he opened his eyes again it was morning, and he felt light and hungry. He moved his eyes to look at the room, really look for the first time. There were the rough walls and high, slitlike windows through which he could see a brilliant blue sky. The candle had been blown out, or allowed to burn down. He lay on a pallet on a raised platform and the only furniture in the room was a large square chest. On it he could see a basin and towels and a large green plastic jar, probably, he thought, containing the evil-smelling balm they had rubbed on him. Finally he looked down at his body.

His left arm was in a splint, his right one blistered, but not too badly. His back felt all right, but there were long, ugly dark streaks across his torso and down into his groin. His legs were the worst; they looked like something that had been barbecued. He tried to move the right one and was agreeably surprised to find that it worked. He started taking inventory—left arm useless at the moment, right one burned but usable. Right leg, left leg—all seemed to be in working order, if not working. He laid his head back. I must live now, he thought. I have something important to do. But at that instant he could not remember what it was, only that it had come to him once, days ago, and would come back.

"WHO ARE YOU?" the priest asked.

He licked his lips and forced the words. "Does it matter?"

The priest studied him. "You must have family, friends. They will be worried about you."

"No," he said, and then, "Who are *you*?"

"I am Lin," said the priest.

"I need water... throat dry," he said, and the priest left at once. He was back in a few minutes with a pottery cup. It was the coldest, most welcome drink he could remember, and he lay back again and watched the priest.

"Where am I?"

"On an island south of Lantau. There is a monastery here, and a fishing village. You were washed ashore almost exactly between them, and a fisherman found you. You have been very near death."

"Was I alone?"

The priest leaned nearer, intrigued by the question. "Yes. Are you starting to remember?"

"Some."

"Do not hurry it," the priest said soberly. "We have heard you moan at night, and cry out sometimes. Your subconscious is helping you keep something in check. It may be best if you think of it a little at a time."

"You sound like a medical man."

"Yes," Lin said. "I am a doctor. My education was financed by my order, and now I work among the people of the island."

"I'm lucky to be here," he said.

"We lack a lot of modern medical facilities and equipment," the priest said, "but we also use many old Chinese medicines and techniques the West has yet to accept. Your burns have been treated with a balm made of herbs that grow on the island. You have had some acupuncture. Call it holistic medicine."

"It seems to be working," he said.

"You are an American?" Lin asked.

"Yes."

"You will need some skin grafts. There is a facility in Texas that specializes in such things. Perhaps you should go there."

"You're knowledgeable."

"Well trained." Lin smiled. "Rest now."

He slept through the day and into the evening. When he awoke again he found he could prop himself up on his right elbow, a relief after the long period on his back. And he was starving. A different priest looked in on him and made the Asian gesture asking if he wanted to eat, a circular motion of chopsticks to bowl to mouth. He nodded and smiled. In a few minutes the priest brought him an enormous bowl of rice, and on the top a long, lean piece of baked fish. He made a drinking motion, and the priest brought him a cup of water, as cold as he remembered, then left the room.

As he was finishing the food, Lin came in, carrying a small stool. He sat on the stool and put his hands on his knees. "Did you enjoy dinner?"

"The best ever."

"You will mend," Lin said. "It will take some time. I must say, you are incredibly strong to have survived." He was silent, thinking. "Technically," Lin continued, "I am supposed to report you to the authorities in Hong Kong."

"Why?"

"For the bullet wound—I see, you did not know about that. Underneath the burned part of your right thigh we found the entry hole of a bullet. It exited the back of your leg, missing everything of any importance. So you have been shot once in the leg, badly burned, and your arm broken. We could be in trouble here, if you are a fugitive."

He knew it was a question. "Not a fugitive," he said. "Not a drug runner, not a gunrunner. Have to ask you to trust me for a while . . . Sorry, hard to talk, still."

Lin stood and looked at him. "I will trust you for now. In time you will have to trust me. Is that an arrangement?"

"A deal," he said, and Lin looked puzzled. "In America we call it making a deal."

"Yes," said Lin. "A deal."

When the priest left he lay back, thinking. He might have dozed a little, for when the thought came back it seemed to galvanize him, and he jerked up on his elbow. It was the same thought he had had days before, the one that he now knew had kept him alive. It was still incomplete in places, for he could not yet remember all he needed to know. But what he did know came in bright and clear: there were some people he had to kill.

"WHO ARE YOU?" Lin asked.

"My name is Richard Casski," he said. "American. Injured in a boating accident. Employed by an exporter in Hong Kong. References at the Hong Kong and Shanghai Bank. A long time in Asia."

"Our deal," said the priest, "did not make allowances for half-truths. But I will respect your obvious needs. Have you remembered everything now?"

"I have," he said, "and you were right. Thank God for the subconscious. And for you, Lin, and all the others here. I won't forget."

"You have been here seven weeks. I would say it is a miraculous recovery. You are very strong. And is your real name Casski?"

"Yes," he said. "In a way."

Lin raised his eyebrows.

"I was an orphan. The classic case, left in a black powder box on the doorstep of an orphanage in Idaho. They gave me my last name after the powder manufacturer, and my first after the manager of the orphanage. Richard Casski."

"Now," said Lin, "what about the rest?"

"Deal or no deal," Casski said, "there are things I can't tell you yet."

The priest sighed. "At any rate, you will be able to leave soon. I saw you walking the island this morning, very fast, too."

"I'm not one hundred percent yet," Casski said, "but everything functions. As long as I have that I can get back in shape."

"Will you go for the grafts?"

"Yes. Soon."

"There's no hurry. It will take some time before grafts are possible. You are welcome to stay here."

"Lin, listen to me. There is something I have to do. It may take months, or years. When it is over I will come back and tell you everything. Deal?"

"Deal," Lin said.

"Any way of communicating off island?"

"Only by boat."

"Is it possible, then, for you to get a message off for me? If you can get to Lantau, you can get on to Hong Kong, right?"

"Yes. We have a system, don't worry."

"I need to get word to someone in Hong Kong that I am alive and well. But no one else should know. Can that be done?"

"It would be better if I do it myself," the priest said.

"Could you?"

"I will go tomorrow. Tell me what to do."

"You go to the office of Tamarind Enterprises on
Connaught Road and ask for the office manager, Mr.
Lee. When you are alone with him, you tell him I am
alive, and where to find me. You ask him to convey this
information to the station chief. And tell him no heli-
copters, no fuss. I want to get off here as quietly as possible. Tell him that's imperative. Can you do that? Good.
I'll give you a description of Mr. Lee and his mannerisms. Don't talk to anyone else, all right?"

"Deal," said Lin.

TWO WEEKS LATER a large trading junk, of the kind that
still occasionally plies between Hong Kong and Singapore, slipped her mooring and headed west out of Vic-
toria Harbor, fighting a crosscurrent and a stiff southerly
wind. The junk was fully manned, and a close observer
would have noted that she was full to the waterline, obviously loaded. From the outside the observer would not
have known that the cargo was a series of boxes weighted
to give the appearance of a heavily laden vessel. Neither
would he have seen the assault rifles stowed in the main
cabin, nor the tall, thick Westerner who kept carefully
belowdecks until the junk was out of the harbor. The
Westerner stayed in the cabin with his charts and sometimes with the junk's squat Chinese captain, the two of
them charting a course and speed that would bring them
into Singapore at night. The big man had a habit of
pulling on his right earlobe when bothered or puzzled,
and the earlobe was red by the time the junk slid around
Lantau and on to the south.

Anyone watching would have seen that some trouble with a mast forced the junk to lie up for a few hours in the lee of a small island south of Lantau. On the shore opposite the junk two men stood quietly, talking in the darkness while a small boat from the junk came shoreward. The two men shook hands warmly, then the taller of them walked to the waterline and climbed, a little stiffly, into the boat, which took him out to the junk. The second man waved until he realized he could not be seen in the darkness. He stood there for a time, while the boat reached the junk and the men in it were taken aboard. He heard the creaking of lines and the sudden raising of a lateen sail, and he saw the junk begin to move. Then it sprang alive, its sails filled. He heard someone calling, in the darkness, and a man's laugh and an answering call, and all at once the junk was stern to and heading away. He knew that by moonset it would be over the horizon.

_____ **TWO** _____

THE ASSASSIN stood in the gray half-light of the still room, listening to his target move about in the bedroom thirty feet away, hearing the target laugh at something the woman said. Very faintly, below him, he could hear movement on the rue de l'Echelle, but only because it was early evening, when the Paris traffic paused for a heartbeat before entering the nighttime rush. A quiet hour. It was the time when his target, the art dealer, liked to visit his mistress before going on to a business dinner.

As he had done many times in the past half hour, the assassin flexed his muscles, doing simple isometrics, keeping his body fluid and capable of movement without delay and without noise. His eyes never left the bedroom as he tensed and relaxed, over and over, staying supple for the killing movement that would soon come. Then he would be back into the crawl space above the apartment's hallway, out along the air-conditioning duct and down to the street. Twice, while the mistress was out, he had practiced that route, and he knew he could do it in the dark.

He would not be followed. The target would die but not instantly and not in alarm, giving him enough time to escape before the mistress screamed and the two burly

men outside the door rushed in, too late. He would not
have hesitated to kill the the mistress and the two guards,
but the assignment was to kill the art dealer, by way of
making a statement. He smiled. The mistress might
complain of the target's diminishing performance, but
by the time she realized what was happening he would
be back in the alley.

He moved his shoulder blades, tightened them, relaxed. He felt the bulge of the weapon in his pocket and
once again touched the bag of ammunition slung over
his shoulder. The ammunition was in a plastic container, covered by a mild-looking green liquid. He remembered all the work that had gone into the
ammunition.

The woman came into his vision now, wearing a short
lace negligee. She sat on the bed and swung her legs up
and said something to the target. The assassin listened
closely, his French not as good as he'd like it to be. He
heard the target laugh again. The woman was a blonde,
not old, not young, and she had been the art dealer's
mistress for years. The assassin had stared at her photograph until he would know her anywhere. He had followed her for days. He had worked out the pattern of the
art dealer's visits. Stupid for a dishonest man to keep
regular habits, but then many such men were stupid.

Now he saw that the woman had shaved her pubic
hair, and that she might be a bit heavier than the photographs had indicated. She sat up in bed and slipped off
the negligee. She laughed, her large breasts shaking, and
put her hands on them, pushing them together and

pointing them at the art dealer. The target walked to the bed, half-clad, and kissed each breast before moving out of sight again.

The assassin shifted his weight to his right foot and back again. He heard the target say something in idiomatic French, and heard the sound of a cork pulled from a bottle. That could mean a longer wait. He shifted again and watched the target come over to the bed, totally nude now, and sit down next to the woman. He handed her a glass of wine. The two smiled, made a silent toast and sipped. A few seconds later the woman sat back in bed and stared at the target. Even from where he was standing the assassin could see the fire ignite in her eyes. She put her glass on a bedside table and stretched out both arms. The art dealer, perhaps a little less eager, took another sip of his wine before setting the glass on the floor beside the bed. Then he moved up the woman's legs, kissing her.

The assassin looked again at the darkening room. He was in a nook off the kitchen, across the hallway from the bedroom. Good that the light was going, but it might make for a difficult shot. As if on cue, the woman said something softly and turned on the bedside light. Then he saw a second light, refracted from somewhere beyond them. Possibly a light in the corridor outside. Still no problem. He thought again of the guards. Let them listen. By the time the woman raised a cry he would be in the Metro, moving across Paris, and nothing would ever, ever connect him with the art dealer's death.

He eased the weapon out of his pocket. The surgical gloves he wore would leave no prints on the weapon, which he intended to leave behind. The gloves would also protect him from the ammunition, which he had to handle. He looked at his watch. He had been in the house, unseen, for more than an hour. It proved the value of his preparation.

He thought fleetingly of the hours he had spent on the problem—to leave him time to get out of the apartment without having to deal with the guards, to make the death certain but silent, and delayed by perhaps two minutes. When he finally realized what he had to do, he went out and bought his weapon at a sporting goods store in Lyons. On the outskirts of Paris he practiced with it until he could either burst a balloon at thirty feet or knock it aside unbroken. He grew to appreciate the accuracy and the silence. Then he told his employers what he needed in the way of ammunition and how he intended to use it. When they stopped laughing, they went to work and produced it.

In the bedroom the woman took her head from the target's lap and lay back, pulling her knees up and reaching for him. The target moved toward her and over her.

The surgical gloves were like a second skin. He had no trouble placing the weapon's brace on his arm and closing the strap with its quick-release buckle. He felt confident, ready. He glanced down at the ammunition bag and pushed it open, gently forcing the lid from the container. Inside were three small ball bearings, all covered in liquid. He pulled one of them from the bag, feeling its texture; it had been roughened by a file to help the liquid adhere to it. They had told him it was the deadliest poison in the world, and certainly suitable for what he had in mind.

In the bedroom the target was moving rhythmically over the woman. He could hear her soft moans and the quickened breathing of the target.

Now.

He placed the ball bearing in the pouch of the weapon and raised the weapon to eye level. He took the classic stance of the duelist, still careful not to make the slightest sound. He flexed again and pulled the weapon back, but not to full draw, not too hard, not too soft. A little penetration of his own.

He sighted and fired.

And remained motionless, waiting.

In the bedroom the target suddenly jerked upright, slapping his left buttock with one hand, then looking at his hand for any sign of blood. It was the way a man might slap at a mosquito.

But only for a second, for the woman was moaning and pulling him back to her. The target rubbed the spot again and looked as if he might have gotten up, but the woman was insistent, and he finally bent to her again.

The assassin moved sideways into the hall, walking on the outer edges of his feet the way *ninjas* were trained to do. He eased down to the end of the hall, pushed the panel from the overhead crawl space and began to pull himself through it. As he started to replace the panel from the inside, he thought he heard the woman's querulous voice.

In less than twenty seconds he was in the alley. He unzipped the jumpsuit and stepped out of it, leaving it on the ground and placing the ammunition bag on it. He took out the weapon and smiled at it and tossed it on top of the jumpsuit. Finally he took off the surgical gloves inside out, folded them and put them in the inner pockets of his conservative, well-cut suit.

He stepped out of the dark alley onto the rue de l'Echelle and turned right, resisting the temptation to step into the splendid bar of the Hotel Normandie. He crossed the street, passed the newspaper kiosk and moved with the people gathering for the entrance of the Metro. He flowed with them down the steps and onto the platform, and it was there that he allowed himself a small but satisfied laugh.

"THEY KILLED HIM with a goddamned *slingshot*," Anderson said disgustedly. "They didn't bother to hide it, either. Left it in the alley." He slapped the report down on the table, the sound echoing in the quiet room. He looked up at the men around the table.

"A slingshot, gentlemen. Let's see you find a case history of that in the goddamned files." He paused for a moment, staring at the offending report, and into the silence came the voice of Rear Admiral Akers, representing military intelligence, the newest member of the team.

"I guess I haven't been here long enough to worry about sounding dumb, so I'll ask the stupid question. What connection did this guy Roget have with the Jihad?"

Anderson tugged on his right earlobe while an air of impending doom infiltrated the room. "You up to speed on the situation reports involving the Jihad, Akers?" Anderson asked quietly. Only those who knew him recognized the edge of steel in the soft voice. Anderson was a veteran of the intelligence wars, the Washington wars, the budget wars and, a couple of times, real shooting wars. He was known to have four-star generals for breakfast, and in this circle a junior admiral was expected to sweep out his own office.

"I read the last sit-rep at midnight," the admiral said confidently.

"That was seven and a half hours ago," Anderson said coldly. "Did you happen to poke your nose into the situation room en route to this meeting? No. You damned well should have. If you can't stay abreast of what's happening here, I'll ask the Joint Chiefs for other representation. And you'll be shoveling shit in Diego Garcia. Clear?"

Akers stared at him, astonished. Then he nodded. "Clear," he said.

Anderson fixed his baleful eyes on each man in the room, in turn: the tall, aristocratic representative of the National Security Council; the subdued Navy officer; the handsome but hard-eyed representative from the Central Intelligence Agency; the nervous gray-haired delegate from the National Security Agency; and finally the quiet man from the White House staff. Each, in his own way, represented years of behind-the-scenes battles, and all of them had triumphed. But in this room they were subordinate to Anderson, who did not hesitate to use his direct mandate from the President.

"I don't have to tell you what we're up against with the Jihad. They started off with the car bombings in Beirut and now they're all over the world, killing people for reasons that sometimes escape us but make sense to them. They're organized, tightly knit and very security conscious, while we, gentlemen, leak like a damned sieve."

He swung his gaze back to the admiral. "I'll fill you in, for the last time. From now on you'd better know as much as I do when we sit here. Roget was the second largest art dealer in Paris. He had ambitions to be the first, so he didn't mind making a little illicit money. So when he was approached by two Middle Eastern gentlemen offering an extremely rare piece of art to be fenced to any willing private collector, he jumped at the chance. He knew damn well that what he was being offered was stolen, and he broke every French law imaginable in agreeing to handle it. What he did, the stupid shit, was sell the piece and turn over to those Jihad representatives only about three-fourths of the money. He cheated them. They don't like that."

Akers cleared his throat and launched a tentative question. "How do we know all this?"

Anderson reached in his stack of papers and pulled out a photograph of a middle-aged blond woman. "His mistress," he said. "She told us everything. She thought she was talking to the French police because we got there first. Are you now going to ask me how we got there first?"

The admiral nodded.

"One of the guards was our plant, a French cop working for us. Unfortunately there was nothing he could do about the killing of Roget. It was a damned masterful job. The killer went right into the girlfriend's apartment and shot Roget in the ass with a poisoned pellet fired from a slingshot across the hall. Quick, quiet . . . and I'm wondering if I detect a slight sense of irony creeping into the Jihad. I mean, it wasn't your usual ritual bombing, right?" Anderson looked for, and got, confirming nods from around the table. He shifted his weight in the chair and waited. It was the CIA man who finally made the connection.

"Are you saying the Jihad has *hired* a killer? Someone outside the brotherhood?"

Anderson stared at him. "Yes."

The tall man from the National Security Council reached into his pocket and pulled out a pipe and tobacco pouch. "How in the world," he asked in a soft Virginia accent, "would you ever run down a man like that?"

"I'm glad you asked, Sinclair," Anderson said, a little meanly, "because that's just what the President of the

United States has asked us to do. Find that son of a bitch and stop him, and all others like him.''

The reaction was gratifying. A quick little shock wave circled the table, and the men suddenly sat forward, the CIA man again taking the lead. "You mean we've got it?"

Anderson nodded.

"Hallelujah," said the CIA man. "It's about time."

Anderson glanced at Admiral Akers. "Don't look so piqued, Akers," Anderson said. "There's no way you could have known about this one, nor you either, Ritchie—" he smiled slightly at the man from the National Security Agency "—we've kept this as tight as possible. But it's here. It's all here."

"What, uh, is here?" the admiral ventured.

"I'll read it," Anderson said. "It's an executive directive, and it establishes something the President wants to call Operation Longbow, to wit:

'By executive directive this date is created Operation Longbow, to employ the resources of the intelligence community of the United States and any friendly foreign nations as available, and other groups and organizations, to nullify the activities of the forces of international terrorism, and especially the Jihad, and to conduct such antiterrorism campaigns and projects as may be necessary to preserve world order and American security. To carry out this mission, Longbow is established with broad authority and sufficient funding to be drawn via secret and special line-item sources within the budget of the Central Intelligence Agency. Those outside the Longbow structure may be tasked to provide such assistance as may be required by Longbow.' ''

Anderson paused and looked up. "It sounds good to me," he said. "Just what we asked him for." He saw assenting nods.

"It goes on to say: 'Facilities, personnel, equipment and other necessary items are to be drawn from appropriate sources via liaison personnel within those sources, whose identities shall be kept closely held. Priority Ultra is authorized in implementation of this directive.' ''

Anderson looked up again. "It concludes by saying this is to be kept from the public, from Congress and from anybody else who has no need to know. I don't have to tell you that if we're going to succeed in nailing these bastards, we'll need a lot of good help and a lot of good luck."

The CIA man's boyish face split in a wide smile. "But we've got the authorization. All the planning we've done can be put into effect. We can start. What's your first move, Andy?"

Anderson sat back and thought for a moment. "Aside from all the organizational bullshit, we need to get started operationally. I think we ought to get people out in the field nosing around. We know the Jihad needs money and support and we know how they're getting it. I'd say the immediate priority is to disrupt them, to put a few wrinkles in their operations before we do anything massive against them. Let's just make a start and maybe rewrite the scenarios as we go, heh?''

"So what's your first move?" the CIA man asked again.

"Hand you the responsibility for setting up facilities. Run the thing out of Langley as we planned. Pretend we're an extension of Special OPs. I leave that to you to sort out and set up. I'm going recruiting."

"Where?"

"Going out to find the toughest son of a bitch I know. I want him with us, and he won't like it a bit. He hates anything that has to be done with a group. Last I heard he was living on a small ranch in Idaho, working it by himself."

"How will you get him, then?"

"I'll promise him vengeance," Anderson said. "Vengeance. He holds a grudge longer than anybody I ever knew."

CASSKI LOOKED at the sections of logs he had just finished sawing, doing it all with an old crosscut saw and disdaining the gas-driven models. He hated gadgets. Even the ax he held now was a two-bladed type that had been around the ranch for years, and as he hefted it he was pleased with its weight, with its old, used look, and with the superb balance that nobody seemed to care about anymore. He bent down and raised one of the sections of the log up on the tree stump, needing both hands to lift it. He picked up the ax again and in a quick, fluid movement, swung it onto the log, hearing the satisfying thunk of it and watching the pieces of wood fall. He picked up one of the two halves and swung again, enjoying the feel of his muscles tightening and the crisp sound of the splitting wood, the sense of real work being done. He could see his breath in the chill of morning, and the old flannel work shirt felt good against his skin.

A man would have to be crazy to leave this, he thought, pausing to stare past the woodpile to the cabin and beyond that to the rail fence and the rolling countryside, the smoke-colored mountains in the distance, sensing the freedom that came with the limitless sky and the silence. It was the quiet that appealed to him most—the absence of engines, voices, things banging up against each other. The silence meant privacy, and safety. At night, in the cabin, he would hear the song of the wind around the corners of the log structure, a natural sound that didn't bother him at all. It was the sound of people he could live without.

Yes, a man would have to be crazy to leave this; yet he knew he would. That knowledge made the day bittersweet and made everything seem more vivid. He was running out of time now. Anderson's message had reached him, and even though he hadn't bothered to reply, he knew Anderson for his stability and his tenacity, but he wished he could have a few more days. Casski stopped swinging the ax and looked at his watch. Anderson would be in Coeur d'Alene now, which meant that before the day was over he would be here, and he would talk, and he would repeat something the message said, which was the only thing in the world that would make Casski give up all this and go back into the maelstrom he had left.

He swung the ax again and the pieces of wood fairly leaped off the stump. Casski knew the frustration would continue for a while, before he got totally immersed in the problems again. As he had so many times in the past, he asked himself why he had ever left the ranch in the first place. And as he had so many times in the past, he answered his own question: the necessity of the job he'd been given. He used to hate the question. Now he hated the answer.

He picked up the ax and an armload of wood and walked to the cabin. The morning had a bite to it; he liked that. On the lee side of the cabin he dropped the wood into the woodbox and hung the ax carefully, blade up, on the pegs of the box. He walked around the cabin and onto the porch and stopped to look in the direction of the road. At some point Anderson would come up that road and change his life again. Well, quit bitching, he told himself; only you can let the change take place and you know you'll do it.

He would not have to psyche himself up for it. He had been waiting for it, for the moment he knew had to come. He had been promised. He was still in physical shape, in damn good shape, in fact, thanks to the ranch work. But mentally he would have to gear himself up to go back into a world where nothing was what it seemed, and the only thing you could trust was the weapon in your hands and *that* only if you were the last one to handle it.

Throughout the rest of the morning he went about his routine, occasionally going to the door of the cabin and looking down the dirt road that led out to the main highway. His roadway, even the ranch itself, was unmarked; Casski didn't need visitors. Anderson might have trouble finding the place, but find it he would, because Anderson seldom if ever went after something he didn't get. At lunchtime Casski took a plate of stew and a beer out to the porch and sat there, eating and drinking and looking toward the highway.

Anderson turned up in the late afternoon, signaling his approach with a cloud of dust that Casski could see from one window of the cabin. He stayed inside while the rental car stopped just beyond the porch and Anderson stepped out, wearing a suit with a short topcoat over it. Anderson put his hands into the pockets of the coat and stood on the far side of the car and waited.

"Anybody with you, Andy?" Casski called.

"Nobody, Cass."

Casski stepped out onto the porch, holding the Winchester. "Come on in," he said.

"I like a man who's careful," Anderson said, walking around the car toward the porch.

Casski watched him approach, a big man, sagging a little from the unused muscles, but a man with no fat on his mind. Anderson was bareheaded and the wind moved small tufts of his white hair as he crossed the distance and stepped up on the porch. He put out his hand and Casski took it, and they stood for a moment studying each other.

"You haven't changed much, Andy."

"A little older, Cass. But you look great."

It was true, Anderson thought. Casski always radiated a kind of controlled ferocity, an energy force that almost intimidated. He was just a shade under six feet tall but so broad he almost looked stunted. His short-cut black hair had just a trace of gray in it, but his face was young. Even so, it was a face that looked as if it had been battered—a nose ever so slightly pushed to one side, a scar above the right eyebrow. The wide gray eyes held the most direct, unwavering look that Anderson could ever remember seeing. The intelligence that shone from those eyes nearly got lost in the overall impact of the power that seemed to flow from the body. It wasn't only the powerful muscles Anderson could see flexing under the flannel shirt, not only the controlled flow of those movements; it was an aura that suggested Casski would be explosive when crossed. Anderson knew it to be true. Casski wasn't just the toughest man Anderson had known. When it was called for, Casski was also the *meanest*.

"Something to keep the chill off?"

"Sure," said Anderson gratefully. "Long trip out here."

They walked inside.

"You didn't have to come, Andy," Casski said. "The message would have done it."

Anderson sank into an old rocking chair that looked handmade. Casski stood before a cupboard and began to make the drinks. He didn't have to ask Anderson what he wanted.

"I thought you'd want to know more, Cass."

"Yeah. But I thought I'd get that in Washington."

"I don't want you to come to Washington."

Casski walked over and handed Anderson the drink. "Mr. Jamieson's finest," he said. "Cheers."

Anderson sipped the drink and looked around the cabin. Comfortable but Spartan. The natural habitat of a man who didn't give much thought to creature comforts. Anderson sat back and watched Casski as the younger man kicked the logs in the fireplace.

"I'll build a fire," Casski said. "Be cold in here soon."

Anderson watched Casski move around the fireplace. He's really at home here, he thought. Casski moved with the sure motions of long habit, and the smell of woodsmoke began to infiltrate the cabin. Anderson took off his topcoat and loosened his tie and rocked experimentally back and forth in the rocker. When Casski finally sat in a chair opposite him, he said again, "I don't want you to come to Washington."

Casski pulled at his own drink, also Irish whiskey. "You'd better tell me everything. Or at least as much as you can."

"It's a mess, Cass."

The older man sat back in the rocker and closed his eyes. Casski waited. Anderson took another sip of the whiskey, and with his eyes still closed he began to talk in a quiet voice, rocking gently. He could feel the fire gathering strength, and he stretched his feet toward the fireplace. "We've finally got our mandate from the President," he said. "People, money, equipment, everything we need. The planning is over, finally, and the damned thing is launched at long last."

"Then why is it a mess?" Casski asked quietly.

"Because it won't be enough. We've started too late. We're playing catch-up and we can't possibly catch up, the way things stand now."

Casski looked at him coolly. "Your message promised me a chance to get even. Is that on, or was it all a false flag of some sort?"

"No, I kid you not. It's a go, and we're all gearing up for it. But it's gonna be a bitch, Cass. We've got to find a bunch of terrorists and put them out of business. And they're quite creative. They kill selectively and in ingenious ways. They're so goddamned sophisticated they stick out like a bunch of sore thumbs in that lot—the rest think the height of creativity is to blow oneself up in a car bomb."

Casski put down his drink, stood and walked to the window. Dark slipping over the hills. Peaceful out there. He turned back to the older man.

"There's some people I want to kill, Andy. I don't care if it's your terrorists or not. I'll choose to believe it is, if you say so, because it's the quickest way I can get back. So let's do it. If it turns out they aren't the people I want, then you're going to hear from me in the strongest way."

Anderson reached up and tugged on his earlobe. "I hear you. But don't worry. It's the same people. Your briefing was graphic, and we know they were in the right time and place to do it. So you've got three faces in mind—"

"And one I don't know," Casski interrupted.

"And I've got their dossiers in my coat pocket. And pictures."

Casski's head came up swiftly. "Pictures?"

"Yeah," Anderson said, playing his trump card. "But before I show them to you we need to talk a little more, work out some understanding."

Casski walked over to the topcoat and fished in the pockets. "You talk," he said, "I'll just make sure."

Anderson smiled. "You don't change much, son."

Casski pulled out the packet; Anderson had wrapped it in a waterproof covering. He took it to the table and sat down, spreading the covering and sliding the manila folder out of the waterproofing. Inside were three sheets of paper, and each one had a photo paper-clipped to it. He spread them out and stared. And stared.

After a while Anderson gently asked, "They the ones?"

Casski looked up and nodded.

Anderson grunted.

"There's a fourth one. The number one. We just don't know who he is, Cass, but we know he's always in the vicinity of those three. They operate like a little cell. A hit team. You'll notice that the Jihad has had no qualms about hiring an infidel or two. Only one of the three is a Muslim."

Casski stared into space, remembering. He had last seen those faces in the middle of an inferno.

"Tell me about it," Anderson said, watching Casski's face.

"I've told you. I told you on the junk. I went over it a hundred times at Langley."

"Tell me again. We've got lots of time, providing the Jamieson's holds out. You go ahead and talk, son. I'll help myself."

Casski sat back in the stiff wooden chair. "We were on John Martin's ketch," he said, "just off Repulse Bay." And all hell broke loose.

THERE WAS A STRONG WIND, but capricious. Martin was at the tiller, his wife with him in the cockpit. Martin was handling the boat easily, with one hand, the other wrapped around a quart bottle of the Singha beer that he preferred to more expensive brands. He was a tall, fair-haired man, gentle and good-humored, and Casski often wondered why he had gravitated to a business that dealt in secrecy and deception. He could have been the affable board chairman of some Midwestern conglomerate, teaching Sunday school and doing volunteer work while his companies employed hundreds of the townspeople, and there would be talk of nominating him for governor. He could have owned acres of Ohio or Indiana or Kansas and joined the Rotary, occasionally taking his wife to farm implement shows or splurging on a visit to San Francisco. Instead he was a spymaster, whose daily fare included wiretaps and double agents, and his wife was not a corn-fed Midwest beauty, but a Chinese woman of a Mandarin family. But certainly a beauty, anywhere.

Li Xixian was of Northern Chinese origin, a tall, proud and graceful woman who could nevertheless unbend and enjoy herself. Martin had had the ketch built for her in a Kowloon shipyard, a double-ender, thirty feet of luxury sailing. Xixian loved being on the water, and more than once had tapped Casski to crew for her when her husband was busy. She was damned good with the boat, Casski knew, as she was with everything. She was older than Casski—about John's age—but Casski was half in love with her anyway. It was a harmless little romantic delusion—John Martin and his wife were the most devoted couple Casski had ever known.

It was Casski's sharp eyes and pure blind luck that saved his life. He was the first to see the dappled pattern on the sea that meant the wind had shifted and was coming from the starboard quarter. He called out to Martin, who waved the beer in acknowledgment and called out an order. Casski started forward, and the first shots struck the mast behind him.

He threw himself down on the deck, calling to Martin at the same time. He heard Xixian scream and something thud along the deck. He heard the sound of a high-performance engine. He started to crawl forward, to his jacket in the bow with the .38 Special in its pocket. He had moved only inches when an enormous force flung him into the air, knocking the wind out of him and hurling him gasping into the water, his head splitting.

Then he was tumbling in the water, disoriented, his lungs on fire. He forced himself to relax and began to rise slowly upward. When he had gotten his equilibrium, he started hard for the surface, expelling air in little bursts.

He broke surface facing the shore and quickly turned around. The ketch was blazing and sinking. He saw John Martin, flung against the fiery bulkhead, but still alive. Even as he watched, the powerboat came back and idled nearby. The man in the bow—Casski could see him quite clearly—casually lifted an Uzi and nearly cut Martin in half.

There was a scream behind him, and he threshed around in the water. Something seemed to be wrong with his arm, but he got around in time to see Xixian swimming for him, stroking and reaching at the same time, her lovely face white with fear. He started to swim toward her, trailing the useless arm. Behind him he heard the powerboat kick to life again. He risked one glance back, saw the boat turn in a tight circle, and knew it was too late.

Xixian screamed again, but the noise of the boat finally silenced her. The boat was practically on top of him. He looked up to see the three men looking down, one of them laughing. The man with the Uzi raised it again and Casski turned to shout a warning. The bullets made little plopping sounds in the water until they reached Xixian, and then they blew away her face.

Casski turned back. The boat was almost within reach. He stroked for it with one arm. If he was about to die—and he didn't doubt it—he'd go out fighting.

Instead the boat backed down, and the three men looked at him. One of them said something to the man with the Uzi and they both laughed. Casski stroked again, and the man at the controls backed the boat again and said something to the other two. Casski could see them vividly.

Suddenly the boat sped off a short distance, then began to circle him. As it neared him, at one point he realized what they were doing and started to move away. The man with the Uzi fired a burst near him and he stopped, treading water. The boat turned in ever-widening circles and he saw the gasoline one of the men was pouring; it spread over the water in broad ribbons. Then he could smell it. He saw the man at the controls turn and laugh, and the man with the Uzi put the gun down to reach into his pocket. There was a spurt of flame and then it hit the water, and the gasoline caught.

He began to swim, but there was nowhere to go. There was another burst of gunfire and his leg twitched involuntarily. The smoke began to rise, and he felt the heat building. The gasoline was drifting close to him. He took a deep breath and went underwater, and knew it was useless. He came up again, flailing, splashing in front of him, trying to drive the gasoline away. As the flames built and the heat began to sear his body, he simply put his head down and started swimming, as hard as he could with one dangling arm. As the flames closed around him he heard, far off, the sound of the powerboat going away.

ANDERSON HAD FINISHED his second drink, and poured a third. He poured one for Casski, too.

"You see, Cass, those are the kind of people we're up against. They've got to be stopped, not just because they hit one of ours, but because of who they are, what they do.

"What I'm offering is a chance for you to nail those bastards and do us all a favor. But you can't go out there like an unguided missile. You need everything—the control, the backup and support, the cover, communications. We'll give you all that, of course. You just go get 'em.''

"You know I'll do that. You knew it before you drove out here, so there's more to it. That's what I'm waiting to hear from you."

Anderson tugged at his earlobe and sighed. "Sure wish I could get you to trust me, Cass."

Casski grinned. "You old fraud. You haven't been trustworthy since you were a ragged-ass second lieutenant. Tell you what—I'll fix dinner while you finish your drink, then I'll treat you to a walk to settle dinner. *Then* you can talk to me. I'm talked out for the moment."

And it was later, in front of the cabin after returning from their long walk, that Anderson told him about the girl.

THREE

SHE AWOKE TO A STILLNESS in the room, and an enormous sense of peace. As she had from childhood, she lay awake and motionless for long moments before moving, letting her eyes move slowly and aimlessly over the rough beams of the ceiling. Then she sat up. She immediately pulled up the down comforter; the room was cold.

Cold, but warming to the spirit. Without getting out of bed she looked straight across the high-ceilinged room to the floor-to-ceiling windows, and beyond them to the peaks and their gentle covering of snow. The morning light was making glints here and there in the snow, and the evergreens stood out against the white backdrop like a child's drawing of winter. Like the winters she had drawn in various hot and strange countries when she was very young, trying to remember a place where there were seasons and snow, and girls could dress up in sweaters and jackets. Her childhood had been long stretches of sand, bottled water, servants, her father's frequent absences, her mother's beautiful face, occasional diarrhea, playmates for a year or two who then left, or were left by her. She remembered nights as warm as days, strange voices and men with turbans, and sometimes, someone who would tease her about being of mixed blood. She hated it then, all the moving and confusion and temporary friendships and sometimes loyalties. And she dreamed of this—quiet, solitude, air that had a bite to it. Cleanliness. Being able to do things for herself instead of sending the houseboy or the *amah*. Privacy.

The room took up the entire loft of the A-frame, and all around her was the warm feel of wood, contrasting with the chill air of the room. She had selected the furnishings herself, paid for them and had them put in place. She loved the beams, the wood, the simplicity of it all. She especially liked the squat, old-fashioned stove, and had a matching one downstairs where the kitchen-living-dining area was a large open room with beams and wide windows. The location of the house, snug against a hillside, gave it a splendid isolation.

She threw back the comforter and walked quickly to a nearby cabinet and slid back the doors. As a concession to the winter scene outside, she selected Sibelius's Second Symphony, eased it onto the turntable and switched it on. Back in bed, she lay listening to the familiar opening strains, and then the elliptical melodies, a lightness and darkness mingling. She thought the music perfectly matched her current outlook—both seemed devoid of people. The music painted a landscape that was uninhabited. Her own past had led her to seek the solitude she had found only by creating this house, in this place; she had decided the house would also be uninhabited, except by her. She would never share this with anyone.

She would, she thought, keep for herself, the real Sue Martin, Tsu-wei Martin, or to put it in proper Chinese fashion, Martin Tsu-wei. The other, the public Sue Martin she would only tolerate—this Sue Martin was merely the breadwinner, the persona that people paid to see and to hear sing. When she was on stage she seemed to disconnect all the wires that tied her two personalities. She just went out and sang, because she was good at it and because it gave her the money to retreat, to escape as she was doing now.

She got up again and padded over to the dresser. She always slept naked, and she felt the welcome chill of the room, the present obliterating the warm and unwelcome past. She had never taken heat well.

In front of the dresser, she stared into the mirror. She accepted the youth as something unearned but welcome; she accepted the body as being good enough, healthy, taller than many Chinese girls but smaller than most Caucasians. She would have been flattered if anyone had told her she looked like her mother—her mother had been one of the outstanding beauties of all time, she thought. Instead she looked like the mixture she was: totally Caucasian at first glance, the Chinese then beginning to show through in subtle ways—the flash of her dark eyes, their slight upward tilt at the edges, something from the steppes of central Asia lingering in the glance they sent. When she sang her hands moved expressively, and a close observer would see an echo of a distant dance coming across the years and the ages. Put her in Chinese clothing in a Chinese village and she just might pass as pure Chinese— But then, she thought, maybe not. She was too conditioned now by the West.

She no longer spent a lot of conscious effort and time pondering her mixed background. She knew she was somewhat exotic as far as the West was concerned, but she also knew there were literally thousands of mixed-blood children these days, the result of East and West meeting in love, in commerce, in rape. And the world was becoming either more tolerant or more used to having them around, because her mixed ancestry created no particular difficulties for her. Sometimes, in fact, it was a decided advantage. Still, she occasionally felt the pull of her Chinese blood. There was nothing about her father and his people that she hadn't learned. Her mother was still a bit mysterious, and she thought that someday she would go back, back to Hong Kong and to old Ah Po, her grandmother, back to Chinese language lessons, back to the friends and the food and the raucous but somehow pleasing sounds of Asia.

She turned to the window.

There was a crack in the gray overcast, and the pale winter sun was dropping through it like a golden liquid, highlighting the snow. It was absolutely still. She walked back to the record player and flipped over Sibelius for the second half, the final movements so full of surprises and freshness. She got back in bed and listened to the music soar through the cabin, watched the sun playing hide-and-seek across the snow-covered hills. As the music climbed toward its dramatic finish, she suddenly heard another sound and sat up straight. Very few people, very few, had her telephone number here. And yet over the sound of the symphony's finale the ring of the telephone slipped shrilly through the room.

I won't answer it, she thought. But she did. And long after she had put the receiver back on the hook she stood staring out the huge windows, no longer seeing the sun and the snow. She simply stood there, staring, unseeing, while the tears formed in her eyes and ran unchecked down her cheeks.

Later she locked the cabin door and walked through the snow to her car. She allowed herself one backward glance at the small, lovely hidden cabin. She didn't know when she would see it again.

HALF A WORLD AWAY, in the heat and humidity of an Indonesian night, Michaelson also stepped from a room and allowed himself one backward glance. He then turned toward the heart of the city and started walking, ignoring the passing tri-sha drivers. In a few minutes his shirt was sticking to his back, and soon his lightweight cotton jacket was becoming discolored with sweat. Never mind, he told himself. It's the tropics. It was also his near three-hundred-pound weight on a frame that should have been much larger. Back in that room the girls had laughed and teased him about his body, but had stopped suddenly when he threatened not to pay. He hated to do that; the girls were so playful, so typically Indonesian in their languor and their absolute failure to comprehend time and their thorough understanding of sex. But one had to be firm when dealing with natives.

There were soft, sibilant whispers in the night, mingling with the ripe odors that told of the nearness of the bush out there, even here in the sprawling city. Jakarta had many places where the countryside and the city seemed to mesh—large plots of trees suddenly intruding on a well laid out thoroughfare, or sudden clumps of what appeared to be pure jungle, popping up for no apparent reason. Michaelson stopped and ran an already soaking handkerchief over his wet forehead. The whispers again, as thin as smoke in the dimly lit streets. What the hell, he thought, he was used to Asian cities at night. How many years had he walked through back streets of backwater ports? He fancied he knew Asia as well as any Westerner. Oh, not that high-level stuff, perhaps. But he knew how to get booze in a place where it wasn't allowed. He knew how many rupiahs he should pay for cigarettes. He could find a store selling penicillin in any one of these pox-ridden places. Two days into a new city and Michaelson was on a first-name basis with the most prominent madame in town. In two more days he could tell you who she was paying for protection.

He stopped at a corner by a small mesh fence and got his bearings. His hotel was the Sahid Jaya and should be—right over there. He pushed off again, and again he heard the whispers behind him for a while. He pulled at a tie that seemed to be tightening the more he walked, and he unbuttoned his jacket to let it flap around him. Again the whispers, and this time he stopped, suddenly chill in spite of the heat. Someone had whispered his name. Not Michaelson, his real name. He wheeled around and saw no one there. A few paces and he heard the name again. He was sure this time, over there to the left. He stepped nearer to a low white building behind a fence, and when he did he heard a footstep behind him.

He flung himself around and came face-to-face with a young, dark man who simply stood there, looking at him.

"Who are you?" he asked. "What do you want?"

"We want you, Mr. Wilson." It was a quiet, deep voice.

"You're mistaken. My name's Michaelson. Excuse me." But when he tried to step around the stranger, he found the man blocking him.

"Your name is Wilson, and you're a double agent, and that—" the dark man started to smile "—is what we want to talk with you about."

Michaelson looked around, trying not to show panic, trying to assess the situation. As far as he could tell there was only the dark man in front of him, speaking a formal and curiously accented English. But the man looked formidable, a tall figure with wide shoulders, and eyes that showed no trace of anything at all. The man might have been looking at a photograph instead of another human being, and it was the absence of emotion in those eyes that brought Michaelson his first darting thrill of fear.

"I'll talk to you in the lobby of my hotel," Michaelson said, "and nowhere else. And my name isn't Wilson."

"Look over my right shoulder, Mr. Wilson, and up to the second-floor window. And then stand very still." Involuntarily he raised his eyes. He saw the silhouette of another man in the window, and also the unmistakable silhouette of a rifle.

"This is monstrous," Michaelson said. "You've got the wrong man."

"Move along, Mr. Wilson."

He stepped gingerly toward the building, the dark man falling in behind him. His legs felt rubbery and his throat was dry. What the hell happened? What the hell happened?

They crossed the street. Michaelson was suddenly very aware of the night and its scents, the smell of *satay* and limes, of faces and flowers. He heard a distant tinkling, like the silver bells dancers held. The dark man gestured up a flight of stairs just inside the building and Michaelson went up, at one point grasping the railing and breathing hard. He couldn't even hear the man behind him, but he knew he was there, all right.

The dark man stopped him at the first door and opened it. Michaelson stepped into a brightly lighted room and looked at its occupant. The man by the window smiled thinly and put the rifle down, leaning it against the inside frame. Because he noticed those things, Michaelson saw the rifle was a Hakim, an Egyptian copy of the old Swedish Ljungman. There wasn't much he didn't know about Swedish rifles, or any other rifle for that matter. But what the hell happened?

"Sit down, Wilson," the dark man spoke. "Over there."

He sat, as lightly as possible under the circumstances. The second man moved closer, and he looked up to see a pair of cold eyes and a square face and a body that seemed to be made out of blocks of metal. The second man didn't speak at all, but turned back and sat on a dingy bed near the window. Michaelson knew he would never make it to the rifle.

The dark man stood over him. "You are a prisoner of war," he said. "You are an enemy of the *Jihadia*, and as such you will be treated with all the courtesies due to a prisoner of war." Then the dark man moved closer. "And then you will be executed."

"Listen—"

"You listen," the dark man said. "You have passed yourself off in Asia for years as Michaelson, but we know you. You began as a gunrunner and then you began to sell to all bidders. We could accept that, it was a matter of economics. But then you began selling information, as well. Knowledge is stronger, Mr. Wilson, than any number of weapons."

"My name is Michaelson—" he began. The dark man hit him, suddenly and hard, right across the nose. He rocked back in the chair and tears sprang to his eyes. He felt his nose starting to bleed.

"You never dealt in the really high-level areas, did you? If you had just kept going as usual we would never have touched you. Two weeks ago, Wilson, two weeks ago in a little bar in Penang you told someone the name of someone who could contact a cousin who knows how to reach the *Jihadia*." The dark man leaned down. "We can't have that, you know."

Michaelson began to sob. "It isn't true. It wasn't me."

"You've played a double game most of your life. We know all about you. Our people could die because of you."

He was crying uncontrollably. "God," he said. "Please." He felt the second man standing, and now the fear reached all the way inside. He could feel his muscles going, felt himself staining his pants.

"Take your clothes off," the dark man said contemptuously.

He lurched to his feet and started removing his clothing. He was stained in sweat, in urine, in fear, and he could smell the terror himself. He didn't care. He only wanted not to die. "Hurry up," the dark man said.

At last his clothes lay in a heap near his feet, leaving him naked. For one of the few times in his adult life, he was ashamed of his body, ashamed for the way they were looking at him. Then he was being eaten alive by his own fear, the body forgotten.

"Into the next room," said the dark man.

"Please," he said. "Please."

The second man picked up the Hakim and pointed it at his groin. Michaelson started shuffling toward the door, sobbing. He felt the door open in front of him and then he was shoved roughly into the room. He looked around, expecting the worst.

The room was bare. It was a totally blank room, windowless and empty, and brightly lit. He stood in the center, shaking with fear, his eyes wet.

The man with the rifle pointed to the far wall, and Michaelson stumbled over to it. "Sit down," the second man said, and he sat.

The dark man then stepped in, holding a cage covered with cloth. Michaelson felt his heart flutter. A moment later the dark man flicked the cloth away and looked at Michaelson with a grin.

"With your experience in Asia, my fat double-agent friend, you must have seen these before." And he laughed.

Michaelson, against all his will and instincts, peered into the cage. And nothing he had known before frightened him as much as what he saw. Before he could reach them, both men were backing out of the room. He heard the cage banging as it was opened and thrown on the floor, heard the two men laughing, saw the light disappear as they flipped the switch. The door swung shut and locked. There was no way out.

He sat there in the darkness, tears streaming down his face. There was no need to run, to hide. It would find him. And the last thing in this life he would look upon would be a small reptile of surpassing beauty—and certain death. Yes, he knew it. He knew the krait was one of the deadliest snakes in the world.

There was no need to care anymore. He stretched out on the floor and let the tears flow. He cradled his head in his arms. And waited.

———— FOUR ————

CASSKI LOOKED DOWN through the window of the jet at one of the loveliest sights he ever hoped to see. A coral island, rising out of the sea like a dream forming, a circle of land enclosing a lagoon made of emerald, with diamond highlights where the sun struck the wavetops, and the waves themselves nudging gently on golden beaches.

"Tetiaroa," the stewardess said, smiling at him. "Your first look at French Polynesia? Beautiful, isn't it?"

He could only nod. Tetiaroa. The name was musical and inviting, but he knew the island was privately owned. There wasn't much, in fact, that he didn't know about French Polynesia. The briefings had been long and deep, and Casski was gifted with the kind of memory that good journalists have—the ability to absorb a lot, in a hurry, and then discard it when the assignment was over. When this assignment would end was anybody's guess. But he thought he knew *how* it would end. It was like hunting vermin in Idaho; you knew something was out there disturbing the peace, but you never knew what to expect.

"We'll be landing soon," the stewardess said with a smile, mistaking his preoccupation. He glanced up and smiled back, then finished his drink and sat quietly through the final approach.

Faaa International Airport was what he expected, a blend of Gallic savoir faire and Tahitian languor. Customs was not unpleasant, and while he waited in line he heard tinkling laughter and looked out through the windows to see graceful bending palms and a cerulean sky. The French authorities in khaki looked almost somber beside the brilliant designs of the clothing worn by the Tahitians. Over it all the warm sun cast a bright patina, and Casski felt himself drawn to the first hint of the fabled charm of the South Seas.

It stayed with him in the taxi as they went through Papeete. By God, he thought, for once the legends may be right. His eyes swept down Pomare Boulevard at the marvelous blend of French and Polynesian, the peaceful coexistence of the waterfront bars and the marvelous old cathedral. He savored it. The rue Jeanne d'Arc, and the rue 22 Septembre, the rue des Ecoles, the avenue du Prince Hinoi—the shops and the bars and the hotels heralding the importance of tourism to Tahiti, and through it all the lingering signs of Old Polynesia; the shops selling *pareu* cloth, the black-pearl shops, the sprawling marketplace where you could buy coconut oil and woven hats, huge papaya and watermelon and small pigs, fresh fish, chicken and bananas. Flowers were everywhere.

More vibrant were the people—saucy Tahitian girls with a swing to their hips that couldn't be duplicated anywhere, he thought. Tall, aristocratic Frenchmen. The French-Polynesian girls, embodying the best of both cultures, with faces like angels and bodies that promised much. Here and there were the Chinese, long-time settlers in Tahiti, and the visiting citizens from middle America, generally favoring bright Hawaiian-print shirts and Japanese cameras. He sat back happily in the taxi while a young Tahitian boy whistled and hummed his way through Papeete and beyond, slipped past the bakeries and service station, past the garrison headquarters, where a bored sentry had adopted an un-military stance, past the Chinese graveyard, and on up to One Tree Hill.

He handed over a generous number of francs and heard the taxi driver laugh and call to the bellboys in-side the lobby of the hotel. He stood under the prowlike roof and glanced around. Hotel Tahara'a—the one with the lobby at ground level and the rooms running down the side of the hill toward Matavai Bay. There was an expanse of green and a walkway up to the lookout. Cas-ski waved the bellboys inside with his bags and went up the walk, through the tamarind trees and out onto the terrace by the wall. Below him the surf broke gently on the black sand of the bay, a haven where the ships of Wallis and Bougainville and Cook had once dropped anchor. Fifteen miles to the northwest another island came out of the sea, wearing a slight tendril of cloud and looking darkly beautiful: Mooréa. Not too far, he knew, would be the scattered beauty of the others—Raiatéa, Huahiné, Bora Bora, Maupiti.

Casski suddenly wished he could enjoy it all.

He turned back to the hotel and went inside, where a lovely Polynesian girl with a delightful French accent welcomed him to the hotel. After checking in, he had his bags sent to the room and walked out onto the terrace by the pool. He had a sense of space and openness, and from the terrace could still see Mooréa, and to his left, the peaks of Orohena and Aorai. He looked at his watch: 1400 hours here would put it at 1900 in Washington. He wondered if he would hear from Anderson before his contact this evening. He wondered what the girl would be like.

In his room he opened the drapes to the view and stepped out onto the terrace, noting that despite the openness he had privacy when he wanted it. He checked over the room out of habit; then he sat down and unzipped his suitcase and began to reassemble the gun from pieces scattered about in various shirts, socks and in his shaving kit. It had been a risk bringing it, and Anderson would have had a fit, but Casski had brought it and now he was glad he had. When he had finished he unscrewed the top of the fake shaving cream, dumped out the rounds in his hand, inserted them into the magazine and slapped it into place. He put the gun under his pillow and lay back to think. After a time he realized there was nothing new to think about and decided to nap. He fell into a restless sleep filled with scenes of fire and noise. He woke up sweating, in spite of the air conditioning.

When he got up it was dark, but warm and humid. The shower helped, and he dressed comfortably in slacks and a loose sport shirt, the .38 stuck into his waistband. He walked down the corridor from his room and into the elevator. No one else was in it. The night had a velvet quality to it, and across the strait he could faintly see lights along the beach in Mooréa; that would be the hotel at Afareaitu, perhaps, or the village at Vai'are—his briefing had been thorough. He stepped out of the elevator and went left into the dining room, which opened onto the terrace. A large, smiling Polynesian boy showed him to his table, and he ordered a double Jamieson's on the rocks.

He saw his contact the moment the man entered the room—a small, dark man, bald but with a bristling macho mustache. Casski knew him to be Turkish, but passing as an Italian. He called himself Morella, and he wore a white suit with an open-collared shirt. He was smiling as he approached Casski's table. The smile was as phony as his name, Casski thought, but stood up to shake hands.

"Nice to see you again, Tony," Casski said.

"Ah, Cass. It's been too long." Morella's voice rang with insincerity. Whatever else, thought Casski, he won't win any Academy Awards.

Morella's grip was as limp as his mustache was strong. A man of contradictions, thought Cass, and one I hate to see involved in this. He would have liked to have a contact he could feel good about. The next instant Morella was sitting and ordering a drink.

"I love American martinis," Morella said loudly, flashing a wide, and this time, sincere smile. "I love America. A great country. But I love France, too. A great country. And nowhere greater than French Polynesia. Ah, Cass, you will love it here." And he looked at Casski expectantly.

Casski leaned close, smiling. "Tone it down. You've got the whole terrace looking this way."

Morella's smile disappeared. "I, uh, I'm sorry."

Casski leaned back and laughed. "Yes, great countries," he said. "And great food. But I don't speak French; would you like to order for us?"

Morella smiled hesitantly. "Yes, of course." He signaled the waiter. Casski, whose French was fluent and idiomatic, sat back and listened while Morella ordered.

"...veloute glace d'avocat à la langouste...filets de sole albert... sorbet des îles... magret de canard au poivre vert et poire en eventail..étoile sauce orange."

Christ, Casski thought.

"...muscadel 'Les Bois Battus' et Baronat St. Emilion," Morella concluded and looked up. The waiter smiled and left with the order.

"Well, my friend," Casski said, "I trust things are going well with you. Your merchandise arriving and departing on schedule?"

"Business is very good," Morella said. "What you call in America, booming. One of the things that makes it such an interesting world is international business. You buy here, you sell there."

"But sometimes it's difficult to make a living that way, eh?"

"Sometimes." Morella nodded. "But then many of us old-time international businessmen are no longer in business, so the competition begins to ease a little."

My God, another one? Too recent for him to have been briefed on it? Casski stared hard at Morella. "Who's retired lately? Anyone I know?"

"I don't think so," Morella said. "A friend of mine in Jakarta, named Michaelson. Just decided one day to call it quits."

"I see."

The food came, and was delicious. Casski ate mechanically, thinking. The Jihad had killed someone in Jakarta he didn't know, but his contact did. Did that change anything here?

"Had you heard from Michaelson lately?" Casski asked casually.

"No, but I heard from a friend of his," Morella said, pouring more wine. "Someone I know, as well. He said Michaelson's health was bad. Very bad. He wasn't surprised that Michaelson had retired, just surprised that Michaelson had so many partners. A lot of partners, in a lot of places."

A double, then.

"Yes." Morella gave a small sigh. "We'll miss him." And Morella tucked himself into his food again, having done his job. I have seen with my own eyes that the big

American is here and safe, he thought, and I have let him know there's been another Jihad assassination. He can take it from there, the arrogant pig.

"Your friend say anything else?" Casski asked.

"No." Morella smiled again. "But I can tell you this— it will be interesting to see who takes over Michaelson's business operations in Jakarta. I think a lot of people would be interested in the job."

"But not you."

"No. Can you imagine leaving all this?"

He had a point. The sky had deepened to a startling blue and the stars were out. Over toward Mooréa there were wisps of clouds, but nothing threatening, and closer in the torches were flaming along the terrace amid the bougainvillea. It was warm but not unpleasant. It was at times like this that Casski became his most watchful. It was beautiful all right, almost unreal; that was what made him mistrust beauty. Beauty was never totally real. It needed a touch of artifice. Casski could understand bleakness, barrenness, space and ugliness. They were real, and they were a part of him now. Since that day in the water, and the flames.

". . . be going soon," Morella was saying. "Anything to pass on to anyone?"

"No."

Morella stood. "Thanks." He watched Morella walk away, then looked around to see who else might be watching. He saw nothing unusual.

He had eaten well but had drunk very little of the wine. Now he ordered espresso and sat, waiting. The show would begin very soon now, on the platform at the end of the terrace. He had a good table, and sat back to wait. The feel of the .38 was reassuring.

There was a sudden hammering of drums, an impossibly fast beat, and the dancers came on—young men with crowns of flowers and boar's-teeth necklaces and loincloths. Then the girls—wreathed in flowers that didn't quite cover their breasts, with long skirts, and flowers in their hair. The dance they threw themselves into was as old as the seas themselves, frankly sexual and also, Casski thought, great fun. Then they began to sing, strange cadences and melodies and interwoven harmonies. Casski thought he might begin to understand why the men of the *Bounty* had a yen to stay in the islands; it was as much an attitude as anything else, and the attitude was expressed perfectly in the music.

The big opening led to another dance, then a slow island ballad, full of sadness and regret. Casski thought he could catch the smell of tiare, or some other exotic flower, but it might have been the poignancy of the song, or the heartbreak in the massed voices. He sat, sipping the coffee, and watched the troupe work its way through the performance for the very appreciative audience. In the short break that followed the excitement of the finale, the stage was cleared of dropped flowers and one of the backdrops was pushed aside to reveal a piano and a middle-aged Caucasian. The pianist began a few tentative notes and the terrace quieted. A young man stepped up to the single microphone and said, simply, "Ladies and gentlemen... Sue Martin."

At last, Casski thought. The daughter.

As the first few notes of the piano slipped quietly across the stage, the girl walked in and took the microphone from the stand, which she adjusted with a very matter-of-fact gesture that held a certain charm for Casski. She followed this by placing the stand to one side and moving near the front of the stage and looking out over the audience. She radiated confidence, Casski thought. And she made no concessions to the audience, no cute greeting. She just stood there and began to sing.

She was, he thought, very, very good. It was a voice that could do opera, with its demanding ranges and need for strength. Yet she sang softly and with candor, a frank and open voice that needed no help from clever arrangements. Casski was struck by her opening song, an old ballad, popular years ago in America and Europe, and it struck just the right balance in this exotic setting. He glanced around to see the audience held by the beauty of her voice, and by the quiet strength in it, and by the selection itself. It was the quality of the voice and the intelligence that seemed to lie behind it that interested Casski most; the girl herself seemed somewhat remote. Certainly she was not your standard nightclub act. No brazen sexuality, no driving rhythms. Just quiet music that made Casski think of the word *competent*. But no, she was better than that.

And she was something to see, this one. Casski, even from where he sat, could find traces of her mother—not only in the face, especially the eyes, but in the gestures, the self-assurance. From her father came the frame that was not oversized but exuded health and vigor. In a half-Asian, half-American blending this one had gotten the best of both worlds. She was a striking beauty, with her dark hair and eyes, her fair skin and good bones and mannerisms reflecting a knowledge of her own looks and talent. Something to see, all right. She might as well be a goat tethered to a log, waiting for the tiger to appear. As he had before ever seeing her, Casski felt sorry for her.

She sang a medley, soft old songs of longing and rejection. She made them sound as if they had happened only yesterday, and that she had been terribly wounded. As indeed she had. Casski believed much of the sadness that she managed to project was real, given what she now knew. He wondered if she was up to what they had to do.

She finished the set and walked away to applause. In a moment she was back, bowing, as if to say *Look at me, I'm dying inside, but I had the good manners to come back and thank you, all the same.* He watched her as she straightened and walked away. She must have known that somewhere in the audience that evening was the man who was going to open an old wound a little more, but she had made no sign, showed no particular concern for her unknown point of contact.

Casski called for the check. He had met his contact and the word would be passed. He had seen the girl, and would see her later, when he was ready. He moved around the tables of the dining room and walked up the slight incline to the lobby, and on to the front of the hotel. Behind him he heard another Tahitian group on-stage, and knew the patrons were stirring out of the mood Sue Martin had created—now they were, probably gratefully, back in French Polynesia. Casski looked up at the flickering stars in the clear and peaceful night. How calm it is here, he thought, how peaceful. He heard a scream.

SUE HEARD running feet outside her dressing room and someone shouting. Suddenly her heart began hammering. They had told her there would be danger, but she had insisted on going through with it. And now, maybe, here it was. Illogically she threw open the dressing room door and ran out. Several people ran past her, heading toward the front of the hotel. She hurried after them. At the front of the hotel a harried night manager was trying, in several languages, to get people back into the hotel, but without much success. She heard another shout to her left and looked up the hill toward the lookout. Then she felt the crowd surge in that direction, and she slipped easily into the flow of it and moved upward. There was a small knot of people already there and they were staring at something in one of the trees. As the crowd neared they seemed to go strangely quiet, and in the silence she looked up into the half-darkness.

A man was hanging there, a small man in a white suit, now darkened and bloody. She quickly turned away, but not before she had seen the bloody horror where his eyes had been. She started fighting her way out of the crowd. Beside her someone vomited noisily, and she caught the stench of it. Her breath was coming fast and there seemed to be people everywhere. She just wanted away from there. She heard a moaning sound, one of the young Tahitians starting to mourn someone he didn't even know. In the sudden silence she felt someone grip her arm like a vise.

"I'm Casski," a voice said. "Come with me."

"Why?" she demanded. "Shouldn't—"

"Come on," he said, sounding angry. "There's nothing to hide anymore. Move it."

"Don't give me orders," she flared. She looked closer. A big man, square and blocky, good eyes, good-looking in a dangerous sort of way. The kind of man she might have expected to be a killer.

He put his face close to hers. "You want to move it along, Miss Martin, or do you want to be carried down the hill? The gendarmes will be here any minute. You want to spend the rest of the night talking to them?"

"All right," she said, her anger still close to the surface. "But you didn't use the procedure. You—"

"To hell with the procedure," Casski said, starting to guide her back toward the hotel. "You want to end up like that mess in the tree? Then let's go."

The crowd was now still, and some of the people had turned aside. Casski glanced up at Morella a last time, knowing the eyes were just a signal, a warning. The death was a promise.

Out in the cul-de-sac that formed the driveway of the hotel they heard the police cars arriving and the police fanning out to preserve the integrity of the scene, and to hold the witnesses. He got the girl past a couple of trees and over a little rise and down to the hotel entrance by way of the side route.

"To my room," he said as they passed through the lobby toward the elevators.

"Why?"

"Because I know where it is, that's all. Why do you ask so many questions?"

"What are you so angry about?" she countered.

"It's my nature."

She preceded him into the elevator and avoided looking at him. They walked in silence down the corridor and stopped in front of his door. He unlocked it and pushed it open. He had left the lights on, and they were still on. He pulled out the .38 and saw the girl's eyes widen. "Stand aside," he told her, and walked into the room. It was as untouched as he thought it might be. "Come on in," he called. "And close the door."

He walked out onto the terrace, leaving the sliding glass door open. He heard her close the door, felt her standing there.

"I think I'm going to be sick," she said.

"The bathroom's to your right." Then he could almost feel her willing herself not to give in to it. He came back into the room and closed the sliding door, and looked at her.

She was more beautiful than the photographs he had seen, and he had seen almost everything that existed about Sue Martin, from infancy on. She was wearing a pale yellow dress with lace in it. She looked a lot like her mother at that moment.

"So you're Casski. Maybe I can get the rest of the story from you now. What's going on here? Did you know that man? In the tree? Was he—"

"Yes, in a way he was one of ours. One of a wide net of free-lancers." He saw her shudder. "A lot of them expect to end up that way, Miss Martin. It goes with the territory, as they say. Sit down, and let's see if we can make this easy for both of us."

She sat and looked at him. He certainly looked able to handle himself. "I'm supposed to tell you some things, and learn some things from you," she began. "I was briefed by a man named Garrow. He told me my parents were killed in Hong Kong. All the time I thought it was an accident. He told me they were killed by terrorists, and that you'd been assigned to help find them. He also told me my father had been in intelligence work all my life. I guess there were a lot of things I was pretty naive about."

"I wouldn't let it bother me."

"But it does. I hate not knowing things." Her chin came up. "I hate not knowing more about you. They wouldn't tell me much. Garrow said you'd tell me what I needed to know, that I was simply to help you. I don't really know what I'm expected to do."

Casski sighed and looked through the glass door toward Mooréa. "Damn," he said quietly. Anderson had told him she'd be the bait. He hadn't told Casski that she wouldn't *know* she was the bait. It was something he was leaving up to the agent in the field, where assessments were often better.

"What are your immediate plans?" he asked abruptly.

"A week here, then a week on Bora Bora."

"Would you consider just going home?"

"Certainly not." She had a determined chin when she was ruffled, he noted.

"Anyway," she said, "there must have been a reason for sending me here, so why would you want me to leave?"

"Because what needed to be done has been done, the people I'm looking for have announced their presence in the area and there's nothing you can do to help at this time."

Sue thought it over. "That means," she said slowly, "that my only function was to bring them out?"

Casski nodded. No dummy, this one.

"Damn it," she said. "All this for nothing? The people who killed my parents are running loose out there. First, all you wanted from me was to bring them out, and then, when they are, as you say, in the area, you want me to go home? What if they just leave, go somewhere else?"

"They'll stay around me now," Casski said.

"Then I'm going to stay close to you, Mr. Casski."

"You'll get in the way."

"Maybe. But I'm going to find these people. Do you have any idea how I felt about my parents?"

"Oddly enough," Casski answered, "I do."

She was quiet for a moment. "You knew them," she said. It was not a question.

"Yes. I knew them very well. You father was my immediate control. And my friend. And your mother was a friend, as well."

"You were close to them?"

"Yes."

She got up and walked to the glass door. He could see her reflection, but not the reflection of her dark eyes. She stared over the terrace and out into darkness for a long time.

"You know they sent me away from Hong Kong."

"Yes, I know."

"They told me I needed a better education. I thought they were just getting rid of me. I was seeing a boy—it was nothing, just a crush—but I thought it was because of him. I wouldn't believe them when they said it was for my own good, for my schooling. They sent me away, crying. I loved them and I didn't want to go. I almost felt they didn't love *me* anymore." She turned to him. "I never saw you in Hong Kong."

"I arrived a few days after you left, Sue."

"They put me on a plane at Kai Tak. I was hurt. And angry. God, I was so mad at them! And it was the last time I saw them. It hurts to remember that."

"I can imagine," Casski said. "But they never held it against you. You couldn't know the truth. They were sending you away for your own protection."

"Then they knew they were in danger? Why—"

"Nothing we could prove. Just a few warning signs, but they didn't want to take any chances. I was sent there in part to help protect them."

She stared at him coldly. "And you failed."

"Listen to me. Your father wasn't the kind of man to stay holed up all the time. You know what he was like—he thought he was indestructible. Well, he wasn't."

She was silent, thinking.

"I guess you did the best you could," she said.

There was nothing he could say to that.

"I'm sorry," she said. "I guess I was nasty."

You are, he thought, a smart-ass kid who has no idea what's really going on here, and despite the fact that you're pissing me off considerably, I can't tell you.

"I think you should get some sleep," he said. "We'll pick this up tomorrow, when everything looks brighter. But you're not going to your room. You take the bed, I'll sleep out in one of the lounge chairs. So just sack out and I'll see you in the morning."

"Are you crazy? I don't even have a toothbrush. And what will the staff think?"

He smiled. "Life is really rotten sometimes," he said. "Tough it out without the toothbrush, and as far as the staff are concerned, have you forgotten where you are? It won't be the first time a girl has slept in someone else's bed in Tahiti."

He heard the bathroom door slam and he closed the sliding glass door gently behind him. It was still a beautiful night. He settled into one of the lounges and put the .38 on the floor beside the chair. She's beautiful, all right, he thought. A lot like her mother, a lot. Her father's stubbornness, though. Damn. He watched the lights winking out on Mooréa, and soon fell asleep.

Inside the room Sue was wide-awake, and thinking furiously. She really had been dreadful, she thought, but then so had he. But here she was, without a stitch on, in his bed, and he was out there like some old Neanderthal man, protecting his cave. Strangely enough, the idea had an appeal of sorts, but she didn't want to think about that too much. And there was something . . . something else he wasn't telling her. It was all too simple.

"ALL RIGHT, gentlemen," Anderson said, "let's get started."

All present, as usual, and all attentive. "Everybody up to speed?" he asked, and didn't wait for the affirmative answers. He sat back and looked sourly at the papers on his desk, and tugged at his earlobe.

"In the classic tradition, there's good news and bad news," he began. "Our man in Tahiti, who happens to be a woman, as you know, watched Morella make contact with Casski. We were right not to jeopardize her. It brought the badasses out of the woodwork but faster than we thought. They killed Morella. I'd say it's gettin' to be damn dangerous to be a free-lancer these days. Casski is fine, and staying close to the Martin girl. I've told him to remain in situ and to be careful."

Anderson paused, thinking carefully about how to phrase the next data. "We have some information on three of the assassins, which I'll share with you. The fourth, as you know, is still a cipher.

"As for the first, his name is Ahmed, six feet and one hundred and seventy pounds, cold eyes and the heart of a true fanatic. He's a Sudanese, draws his inspiration from another, earlier resident of Khartoum, the Mahdi."

"The what?" asked Admiral Akers.

"The Mahdi. A Shukri belief is that a second great Prophet will come to the earth, in the tradition of Mohammed—a Mahdi who will lead the people closer to God. If you'll remember, the Mahdi and his followers, in the late 1880s, launched a series of raids against an oppressive government. The British, with their visions of empire still intact, even though the empire wasn't, sent Chinese Gordon to Khartoum to quiet the natives. The result was that the natives kicked the living shit out of the forces loyal to Gordon, took the city and took Gordon's head. The Mahdi died soon afterward."

The tall man from the National Security Council, Sinclair, leaned forward. "And this Ahmed is inspired by the Mahdi?"

"He might even think he's being personally guided by the spirit of the Mahdi," Anderson answered. "It's an idea that won't go away—the thought that out there somewhere is a young native boy who will rise and lead all the faithful back to God and away from contaminating influences. The appeal is that the Mahdi won't necessarily come from a ruling class—he'll be some poor peasant boy—and to be the Mahdi requires a life of purity and virtue—and then be chosen by God, of course. What I'm getting at is that the only requirement to be the Mahdi is to be male, Muslim and picked by God. It could be anybody.''

The admiral stirred. ''Are you saying he thinks he's a new Mahdi?''

''I don't think he does,'' Anderson said. ''But he believes in the idea, and in the type of rebellion the Mahdi preached. It has an engaging simplicity, gentlemen, and that is: kill enemies, for they are also the enemy of God.''

''What else?'' Sinclair asked.

''I'll give you dossiers, but basically he's cunning but poorly educated. He's single, never married, spent his life learning weaponry and fixing on all non-Muslims as possible targets. Somebody said that one man's terrorist is another man's freedom fighter; this one considers himself a freedom fighter. And he likes to kill.''

Anderson let the silence drag out a bit, waiting for questions. He reached out and picked up a second file and opened it, staring at the face that glared back.

''Our number two also has a name, although it may not be the one he started with. We aren't sure about the pseudonym but it doesn't matter anymore. He's spent his life as Yuri Kopalev. Big and tough, Russian father, mother unknown. We're pretty sure he's a product of the terrorist training center in Moscow, and it could be that he met Ahmed there. They're about the same age. And they certainly have the same inclinations. Kopalev, though, isn't your typical idealistic Russian patriot. He's also a terrorist because he likes it, and he's always hated being poor. Now he's well paid.''

"Kopalev is an expert with just about everything that you can name that's used to kill people. He's probably even invented a few methods. He was briefly a low-ranking officer in the KGB, but was drummed out for stealing. We don't really know how he'd be received in the motherland today. He's been out of Russia for years. More details in his dossier, but you get the picture.''

"And the third—'' Anderson picked up another dossier ''—almost required a wide-angle lens just to get his picture. He's Chinese, damn near a giant. His name is Wu Kwai-sen, and he's just a bloody big tough kid from Shanghai's docks who'll do anything you want for money. He's got all the requisite credentials—early training in wu shu, the Chinese martial art; early training in murder, because he did some time for killing a girl; and some early training in rape, arson and robbery.''

Sinclair asked, "How did they all hook up?''

"Ah,'' said Anderson, "that's a key point, and one we don't know.'' He peered at Sinclair. "That's part of what this is all about, you understand.'' Sinclair nodded.

"Let me get this straight,'' the admiral said. "We have a team of four killers, hired by the Jihad as assassins. Your man Casski knows three of them, and he's out looking for them. You've put the Martin girl out as bait—'' The admiral paused. "Why?''

"Because,'' Anderson said, "we leaked the word to the Jihad that she was her father's insurance in case anything happened to him. They believe she knows most of what he knew about the Jihad, which was considerable, so they'll want to get rid of her, if possible. Now we've got Casski close to her in hopes they'll come out of the woodwork—at least one of them. Casski was with Martin when he and his wife were killed, and has his own motives for wanting to find them. Between the two of them they'll turn up something. And if the Martin girl is caught, she knows so little about us she can't cause any damage." Anderson let the implication of that sink in. "Of course, we're hoping it all goes well, and they don't grab her."

"Of course," said Sinclair, with a trace of irony.

"How did you get word to the Jihad?" the admiral wanted to know.

"We told a man named Michaelson; we were pretty sure it was information he would want to sell. He obviously handled it unwisely."

Something had been moving around in the back of the admiral's mind, and he finally got a grip on it. "Why," he blurted out, "hasn't the Jihad come after the girl before this?"

"She's been in school, under a false name. When we realized she had a genuine talent, and when it became clear she could pull these people out, we helped launch her career. She doesn't know that. We did a lot of hype for her, packed some clubs, just to get her going. As you know, all this is very recent. I heard her sing, though. Pretty damn good. I'd say she'll make it on her own, and very well. Anything else?" The room was silent.

"All right," said Anderson, and watched them leave.

He sat there a long time after they were gone, thinking. They were, he reflected, a good group of men, typically American in their outlook, patriots all. This terrorism stuff was nasty business, and they really hadn't the background to come to grips with it. They hadn't, for example, asked the most obvious question because it probably was too obvious, and they were seeing through it. Well, they'd all know soon enough, providing Casski was up to the job, and he certainly was motivated. Casski. If only they could keep Casski and the girl alive long enough.

"Christ on a crutch," he said aloud, and tugged on his earlobe, and sat there for a time, bemused by the sound of his own voice in the empty room.

HALF A WORLD AWAY, Sue and Casski were ordering breakfast on the terrace of the Hotel Tahara'a, Sue struggling with French, Casski enjoying himself in Tahitian, and the large, smiling waiter laughing at them both.

"*Café au lait, s'il vous plaît*. . . and, uh, *oeufs à la*. . . *à la*. . . damn. . . oh, I've got it. . . *oeufs à la coque*." She sat back and smiled triumphantly. It was, Casski reflected, one of the nicer smiles. She had a beauty that could be distracting, but there were times when she was very girlish and easy, very open. He liked her that way, unaffected. He suspected she was that way more often than not, but this business was getting to her.

"Taofe pai," he told the waiter, showing off a little. Casski knew he was quick with languages. *"E piti huoro moa farai pani . . . saisis. Maururu."*

The waiter laughed again and said in clear English, "Very good, sir," and went away with the order.

"I don't know how you do it," she said. "I struggle with languages. You've been here a day longer than me and you're ordering breakfast in Tahitian. You have other talents I don't know about?"

"None to speak of."

"Except modesty."

"Deserved."

"Cass—can I call you that?—is there anything about this you aren't telling me? We've been very close to each other the past few days and I'm getting to know you, but I think you're holding out on me."

"I'll tell you this much," he said. "I think our nasty friends are getting a little restless . . . just a feeling I have. I think whatever they do, they'll try it soon. Running out of time in Tahiti, though, aren't we? Your Bora Bora engagement starts tonight. I think that's when we'll have to be careful how we play it."

"You'll be on the same flight."

"Yes."

"But you know them. You'll be able to spot them if they show up."

"Yeah, that's for sure."

"How do you know what they look like?"

"I'll tell you that later. Enjoy your eggs, and look at that scenery. That's Orohena there, more than seven thousand feet. And I'm sure going to miss that view of Mosuréa across the strait." He sat back with his coffee. "When we fly out today I'm going to give you a little room. It's just possible they're more interested in me than you at this point."

"I don't know why they're interested in me, anyway. Father never told me *anything*. I thought he was some sort of foreign service officer."

"But they don't know that. Come on, let's get you packed. I'm going to take you to the plane, then do a little slow fade. But I'll be there if you need me."

Through the morning he was close to her, and when she checked out in the early afternoon he was nearby. He rode in the same van to the airport and went in front of her through the domestic gates to the aircraft flying them up to Bora Bora. It was a hot, windless day, and when they were airborne he could see the sunlight drifting through the aircraft windows. Sue sat a few rows in front of him, and he ignored the islands floating by underneath the wingtips—Huahiné, Raiatéa, Tahaa—and watched her closely. If there were killers loose he didn't recognize or know about, he wanted to be ready when they made their move. It wouldn't be in the air, though. He was now pretty sure it would be on Bora Bora, because of the few days of inaction.

Just under an hour after takeoff they winged over Bora Bora, and he looked down at what he had read was simply the most beautiful island in the world. He believed it. In that vast blue ocean, the calm green lagoon was encircled by jewellike *motus*, and on the irregularly shaped island itself he saw a towering massif that he knew was Otemanu, and another one behind it, Pahia. Names from the French map he had seen leaped out at him: there were the two bays, Baie de Faanui and Baie de Poofai, and the outer *motus* of Mute, and Manini, and the southernmost point, Pointe Matira.

They flew straight in to the airstrip on Motu Mute, the first airstrip in French Polynesia, built by the Americans during World War II. The sense of wonder stayed with Casski as the plane rolled to a stop and he stepped down onto everyman's dream of the South Seas.

He was struck by the sense of languor, the feeling of peace. He had an impulse to take off his shoes and shirt, and wasn't surprised to see some of the women removing their shoes to walk in the sand of the *motu*. He watched Sue standing with a soft smile on her face, shoes in hand, pushing her hair back with one hand and looking out over the water. Among the passengers there was no one else he recognized, except an elderly British couple he had seen at the Hotel Tahara'a. In a few minutes the baggage was unloaded and two young Tahitian men were ushering them toward the boat.

He saw Sue safely aboard and stepped onto the ferry after her. It was a large, airy, serviceable craft and it pushed off only a few minutes late, exceptional time by Tahiti standards. In a few minutes they were crossing the lagoon, and soon working between Tevairoa and Pointe Tereia, then on past Motu Ahuna and Pointe Farepiti. The lagoon was dotted with boats, some small canoes without sails, others graceful, gull-winged outrigger canoes. Occasionally he would see a larger yacht, up from Tahiti, anchored in the flat, clean waters. When they passed Pointe Pahua he got his first glimpse of the village of Vaitape, small but spreading along the contour of the beach. As they closed on it, he saw the dock and the curio shop, and beyond it the village itself.

As expected, there was a greeting from the Hotel Bora Bora, and a special delegation for Sue. Most of the passengers piled into *le truck*, a charming, creaking converted truck, which would take them to the hotel. For Sue, due to open that night, there was a battered but serviceable Renault and a smiling Caucasian representing the hotel. With him was a young Tahitian man, who placed a wreath of shells and flowers around her neck. Casski saw them talk for a few minutes and gesture toward the car. Then she looked around for him, an oddly touching gesture of vulnerability. She caught his eye and he nodded and she got into the car. Casski got into *le truck* and sat next to a large, sweating woman who tried unsuccessfully to talk to him.

The Hotel Bora Bora was situated on a point near the southern end of the island; it was a collection of bungalows and service cottages and an enormous, open dining room where Sue would sing that night. As he checked in he looked at the possibilities and was worried immediately. Anyone, out there in the dark, could get an angle on her from almost any direction. Even inside the large room, there were scattered tables all circling a platform. He saw a mezzanine arrangement where there were stage lights. As he watched, she was escorted into the manager's office to the left of the lobby, and he waited until she came out again. She stood for a moment, looking into the window of the lobby boutique, giving him time to approach.

"Your bungalow?"

"Over the water, the last one to the right."

"All right, fine. Do a little shopping and let me look it over first. Give me say, twenty minutes." She nodded. "Meanwhile, stay in the boutique. I'll come back for you."

The bungalow was one in a series, each with its individual pier, out over the waters of the lagoon. It was a single-room structure with a woven pandanus roof and rattan furnishings. Casski had no trouble getting in because the door was open and a smiling maid said, *"Ia orana oe,"* and he answered her the same way. While she continued to work in the room, Casski stepped out onto the wooden decking. There were steps that led directly into the water. The next bungalow was a good fifteen meters away. It was all right, he thought. This was where they would come for her, because it was so perfect. He knew just how he'd do it himself, if that were the assignment.

He went back to the boutique, where she was buying an eyelet shirt. "Why are the shirts full of holes always the most expensive?" he asked her, and waited until they were out the door. He walked with her down the path, through the grove of palm trees toward the bungalow. "I'm in a bungalow called 'Orare' not far away. You'll be all right during the performance. When you're finished, don't delay in the room—come on down to the bungalow and get settled as quickly as possible. Turn out the lights in your room. I'll be there, but just ignore me. Don't talk to me or acknowledge me in any way. All right?"

"They'll want me to have a drink after the show," she said. "They usually do, it's their way of being hospitable. I'll be down as soon as I can."

"Plead a headache, then have one of them walk you down to the bungalow. Tell them you've got bad night vision, or a lousy sense of direction. Anyway, get an escort. I'll be in the room already."

"Got it," she said. "Casski?"

"Yeah?"

"Will it be all right?"

"Sure. Don't worry." *Let me worry.*

They reached her bungalow. "Did you ever see anything more beautiful than all this?" and she gestured toward the lagoon. And then she was in the bungalow, and he turned away toward his own.

THE ASSASSIN STOOD very still in the faint shadow of the pilings of the bungalow. Night had dropped like a weighted curtain, but it brought out brilliant stars, and there were still lights along the beach, from the torches. He could hear music, too, no longer from the room where the woman, Tsu-wei Martin, had performed, but spontaneous music on the beach outside the dining room. Tahitians, he thought, they think life is nothing but music and dance. He had never danced, not once.

And music, music belonged to another world. This was his world—the silent killing, at night and unexpected. He knew of no one who could do it better.

He waited by the pilings with great patience. Several times he had had the opportunity to kill the woman, and perhaps the man, Casski, as well. But there were certain requirements now. After he had killed that fool Morella, there had been a great outcry on the island. He had forgotten how small these places could be. He would kill the girl now and make it look like an accident. Casski would come later, some other time and place. They had told him the girl was the more important target.

He listened to the sounds of the night. There were strange birds resting in the trees along the shore, filling the night with their cries. All around him the waters of the lagoon were washing up against the pilings, the water still warm from the day's sun. He had the landman's instinctive dread of the dark waters stretching in front of him, but he also knew it would be the easiest approach. And he was the logical one; Ahmed, a product of the desert, couldn't swim. Wu was just too big. He smiled to think of Wu coming out of the water like a beached whale. He would make so much noise he'd alert the whole hotel.

Kopalev stayed on by the pilings until the noise subsided on the beach. He looked at his diving watch. It was shortly before midnight. The manta ray that usually put on a show just beyond the bungalows would be gone by now, because the lights were out and his prey, attracted by the lights, would have gone elsewhere. He was glad he had come to Bora Bora a couple of days early, to get the layout of the place. Besides, two killings close to each other in Tahiti could have caused the gendarmes to look more closely at everyone coming and going.

He thought over his course of action. He would slip into the girl's bungalow by sea, drug her and bring her back into the ocean, where he would drown her just beyond the bungalow. It would be assumed she had gone for a late swim and run into trouble. Odd how, at times, you had to come back to basics. He could kill with a great variety of weapons, but tonight he would use one of the most elemental of forces, the world's largest ocean. Five more minutes.

He wasn't thrilled about the prospects of getting out there himself. Yes, it was a safe lagoon, but it was dark, and wet, and filled with creatures better equipped to live in it than he was, and he did not care for that situation. From his earliest days, those hard, cold, poverty-racked days in Skovorodino, he had wanted to be safe and secure, and the only way that could be achieved was to be either rich or feared.

He took a last look around and slipped out from under his own bungalow, getting low in the water, which had become surprisingly cool. By the forward piling he stopped and put on the fins he had checked out from the supply cottage. He was wearing swim trunks, a dark blue T-shirt and a face mask. In a waterproof pouch in the zippered pocket of the trunks, he had the gauze stained with chemical. It would put her out like a light, and then he would put her out forever.

With the fins on he eased down into the water, just his head showing. Moving slowly he pushed out into the mild current that flowed from around the point, and let it carry him along the row of bungalows until he could swing in at the last one. He noted with satisfaction that everyone in the other bungalows seemed to be sleeping. At least their lights were out, and that was all he needed.

He felt a fish bump his calf and resisted a sudden, panicky urge to thresh his leg. Nothing in this lagoon could be harmful. He had to keep control. The current was stronger than he thought and he hardly had to move at all—just keep his position near the bungalows and glide past them with an occasional gentle movement of his fins. Nothing in the lagoon could harm him, but he did feel more secure with the diving knife strapped to his right leg below the knee.

There it was.

He did a quick calculation. To climb onto the steps with the current behind him would be less noisy than approaching from the other side. But first, a little reconnaissance. He turned in the water and let it push him up and under the Martin woman's bungalow.

He held on to one of the large pilings on which the bungalow rested. He looked at his watch. He would wait, and listen, for fifteen minutes, then he would move. He waited by the piling and was pleased that his heart was steady and his pulse regular. He took pride in his work, because professionalism was a refuge.

He swung to his left and went out into the current again, and with his right hand caught the last of the three underwater steps. He eased gently out of the water, moving ever so slowly. He sat on the third from last step, slipped off the fins and put them above the waterline. With his hands he pressed the steps above him, listening for squeaks, testing their reliability. Then he climbed them on his hands and knees.

When he reached the level of the terrace decking he stopped and looked. It was very dark, the nearest light coming from far down the beach. If he couldn't see he couldn't be seen. He straightened up and stood still while the water ran off him in little rivulets. Moving on the outer edges of his feet, as he had been taught, he eased up to the door.

She had left her sliding glass door open, as most people did here, and had simply closed the screen. He tested it, and smiled to find it also unlocked. He would never go to sleep in an unlocked room. He inched the screen door open and waited again. Then he dropped silently on all fours and moved slowly into the room toward the bed.

He could hear her breathing, a little irregular. He suddenly wondered if she were really asleep. But why not? He waited again. He eased the zippered pocket open and took out the pouch, slipping the gauze out of it. The chemical smell hit him immediately, and he held the fabric at arm's length. He put the pouch back in the pocket with one hand, then with both hands unfolded the wet gauze. At last he stood up, and stepped quietly to the side of the bed and looked down at the woman.

He was reaching for her when something hit him like a truck.

The gauze flew away and the momentum of the attack hurled him back past the bed and through the door. He hit the decking with a thud that made his teeth rattle, and then his training took over. He brought up his knees and threw a punch, all at the same time. It was a man above him, a strong shadowy man. The punch hit something solid but seemed to do little damage. Then he felt the man's hands around his throat. He threw his knees up hard and felt the man react. Kopalev grabbed for the diving knife and felt his arm caught in a vise. He twisted and turned but there was no escape. He felt the stirrings of fear; the man above him was strong, the strongest he had ever known.

The fear gave Kopalev strength. He put all he had into a mighty push and felt the man roll away. But when he tried to get to his feet the man was back again. Kopalev tried to think, and finally decided the knife was his only way out. He took two hard blows in the stomach and ignored them as he reached again for the knife and finally got it. The other man rolled away and Kopalev struggled to his feet, only to have the dark shadow on him again. He dropped the knife low in his right hand, as his adversary closed, then Kopalev swung the knife up, viciously.

He felt his right arm go almost numb. The bastard had blocked it! The assassin stepped back to swing again but the man was on him again, and he felt his nose break from a knife-edge slash from the back of the man's hand.

Kopalev staggered back and felt the edge of the wooden railing, used it to propel himself at his attacker. He swung the knife again.

There was a blow on the side of his arm and his elbow bent and then the shadow was on him again, strong and fast. He felt the knife touch his chest, felt the weight of the other man slamming against him, felt the knife sink deep into his own body.

Then he was standing alone, his hand still on the hilt of the knife. There was a fire in his chest, a volcano, a violent eruption of pain. The shadow stood before him, waiting and watching. The fire turned to cold, like nothing he had ever known, would ever know again. He felt the stars turning, the world spinning. He felt himself falling, and the last sensation he knew was the weightlessness he felt in the embracing water.

It's so dark, he thought.

ANDERSON SAW no reason not to be jubilant. "He did it, by God," he told the men around him. "Scratch Kopalev."

"And then there were three," Sinclair said. "Is Casski all right? And the Martin girl?"

"All right." Anderson smiled broadly. "Both of them, all right. I told you Casski is tough. And mean. He was complaining to me. He wished it had happened in the daylight so he could see Kopalev's face—and Kopalev his."

"He probably had an idea, didn't he?" asked the admiral. "After all, that was the assignment."

"You've a remarkable capacity for the obvious, Admiral," Anderson growled, but not even Akers could dim his satisfaction. Casski was enjoying at least a moment of success, and against all odds. Anderson pulled on his earlobe.

"What was the next move?" somebody asked him, and he came back to reality with a start. He had been thinking of Casski, of the way he had seen him after the fiasco with the Martins, Casski burned and broken but recuperating, and building the kind of hate that could fuel a man for a lifetime. He thought of Casski's eyes that night, there in the cabin of the junk. He wondered if Kopalev had, after all, seen deep into those eyes.

"The next move," he said, "is a change of venue. We get Casski and the Martin girl out of there." And he waited for the follow-up question that he was sure would come from Akers.

"Why?" asked the admiral.

"If we leave them there it will look like we're baiting the trap. Kopalev's death will make them suspicious enough. They'll have trouble believing that Casski simply beat him. They may think we've got a battalion of Marines on the island, or some such. I think it's best to move them soon, a day or two at most. So we find the Martin girl another engagement if we have to, unless something turns up for her. And it well may—she's a genuine talent."

"So we do nothing for a day or two, heh?" Sinclair asked.

"Lie doggo," Anderson said. "Sometimes it's the best thing to do."

CASSKI SAT on the terrace, thinking murderous thoughts.

Beyond the bougainvillea, beyond the beach, lined by a stretch of sea, Mooréa sat on the horizon and looked even more appealing by moonlight. I should be content with the moment, Casski thought. Will I ever learn to loosen up again? She might have been reading my mind a moment ago when she told me to relax.

"It's pretty much over, isn't it, Cass? I mean, they won't bother anymore, will they?"

He turned to her. She was on the lounge in a *pareau*, already tan. He could see the fold of the garment, giving him a look at nice legs. In the moonlight he could see the white of her teeth, but there were shadows when he tried to see her eyes.

"Is that what's important to you?" he asked nastily. "Not being bothered anymore?"

He heard her sigh. "We've been through it enough, haven't we?"

Granted. In the hours following Kopalev's death she had alternately clung to him and pushed him away, relieved and frightened for his safety as well as hers. In those hours between Kopalev's final splash into the lagoon of Bora Bora and the coming of sunrise, she had sat weeping in relief and lashing out in defiance. He had just let her go, let her work it out for herself.

When she did, she was livid. "I don't want revenge this much," she said.

"I didn't expect Martin's daughter to be afraid," he lashed back.

"You bastard, it's not for me." It had brought him up short then, that he had misjudged her so badly.

"I don't want you to get killed, Casski. I can't put it any simpler," she said through the tears.

"I won't, dammit. And I'm not through yet."

The argument had gone on intermittently throughout the morning and into the afternoon, when they were waiting at Vaitape for the launch to take them out to Motu Mute for the flight back to Tahiti. They took separate taxis back to the Hotel Tahara'a, though he was careful to keep close behind her. At the hotel he arranged a room nearby, and after separate dinners he finally asked her over to his terrace for a drink. She had accepted, in a mood that was clearly conciliatory. It was his own damn fault that he couldn't lighten up at the moment. But what he really wanted was for her to realize that the danger hadn't passed.

"So you want to keep killing them until one of them gets you," she said quietly. "And for all we know they've spread your name and photo from here to Beirut and back. There's one of you, and no end of them. Can't you see that?"

"I've considered it," he said truthfully.

"But you won't stop."

"I don't think it will work that way. What will happen now is that the rest of them will decide they have to do it themselves. They can't go running back to their masters and ask for help. They're supposed to be the professionals, the top guns. It's a matter of pride and caution—they *want* to do it themselves and they more or less have to, or admit they aren't the last word in style, dash and color that they think they are.''

"I see," she said, and grinned. "We've got them surrounded."

He liked to see her in such moments. The grin she flashed was easy and infectious, and it took the guarded look out of her face. That look was new, he thought, brought on by Anderson telling her about her parents, and all that had happened to her since. But when she smiled like that all the cares dropped away and it was impossible not to respond. Sometimes—and he had to admit it now—when he was alone with her there was a certain arousal, something he fought down in his mind. He still thought of her as Martin's daughter, not entirely a person in herself, and he thought that if he analyzed the situation long enough there would be a reason he felt that way, but he didn't want to think about it too much. He had enough to do.

"You're awfully quiet, Casski."

"I don't talk a lot at the best of times. You must have noticed that."

"That . . . and other things about you."

"Umm."

"You're smarter than you look," she continued. "Not that you look dumb. You've really good eyes. You're obviously competent. There's a mean streak in you, too, isn't there?''

"How would you know?''

"You liked killing Kopalev.''

He looked up, watching her. "What if I did?''

"It makes me a little uncomfortable, sometimes.''

"Do you remember who he is? What he did?'' He could hear the harshness in his voice.

"I haven't forgotten a thing,'' she said coolly. "And I'm not sorry he's dead. I think I am sorry that you enjoyed killing him.''

"I see,'' he said. "It puts me in their class.''

"Not exactly. It's hard to explain, Cass.''

He turned on her, some of the tension rising in him at last. "Learn to live with it until this is over,'' he told her, his voice hard and flat. "I'm going to capture or kill every one of those sons of bitches, and then I'm going back to Idaho, and you can go wherever the hell you want. All you're asked to do is stay visible until they all come out of the woodwork—not exactly an intellectual exercise. I wasn't sold on bringing you into this, anyway, but you're here, and you'll do your job.''

He turned and looked at Mooréa. He heard the door slam.

FIVE

"YOU MUST REMEMBER," said the old Chinese man, "that we are the keepers of order. Have some more dim sum."

"Thank you, Honored Uncle," Wu replied, and, for a man of his enormous size, wielded the chopsticks gracefully as he picked up another of the small, delicate shrimp-stuffed dumplings. The old Chinese watched him approvingly. Had this mountain of a nephew turned out to have bad table manners, he would have dismissed him by now, in spite of his curiosity. His elder brother's son obviously came with a mission and they would get to it in time. But for now it would amuse him to instruct this young man in some of the intricacies of Chinese behavior. Along the way, he would learn what he wanted to know.

"Order," said the uncle. "In any nation where there has been a strong Chinese community, it is we, the Han, who have maintained the most stability." Wu noted the use of the word *Han*, the traditional and classic way of referring to a true Chinese person not of the minority groups that comprised a great deal of China.

"Please continue, Honored Uncle," Wu said, catching the gleam of appreciation in the old man's eye. Patience, he told himself.

"We have been here for centuries," said the old Chinese, and made a vague gesture with one hand, a gesture that seemed to sweep away the walls of the small room, and extend beyond, to all of Southeast Asia. "We came here thousands of years ago, fleeing from persecution, finding only more persecution. Yet we remembered that we were chosen. By thrift, by filial piety, by our sensible knowledge of commerce and trade, by our reliance on family, we survived not only here in Thailand but in many other places, as well. In surviving, we brought a sense of stability." He paused and turned his narrow eyes on his nephew. "Do you know what we were called?"

"No, Uncle," Wu said.

"*Hua Chiao*—the sojourning Chinese. I leave you a few moments to think about what that means."

Wu sipped a little wine, a delaying tactic as he thought of what to say next. He needed this old man, and there was no rushing him.

"I would think, Uncle," he said at last, "that it means the Han were different from all others around them in their approach to business, to life."

The old man regarded his nephew. A cautious answer, he thought, but not inaccurate. He reached out and gently picked up another dim sum. "As Han, we were already different from all others," he said, and having delivered the gentle rebuke, he began to enlighten his nephew.

"Once we could do business only in the backwater villages of Indochina. So we concentrated on small businesses, particularly in agriculture. When we became too rich for the villages we began to quietly buy property in the cities, adjoining other Han. We expanded into mining then, and into transportation. In time we were doing business from the back seats of Mercedes and Daimlers. And then we were into banking and finance."

Wu studied his uncle's face. It was lined with deep indentations, wrinkles pronounced enough to be mistaken for scars. The man's eyes were mere slits. His voice gave nothing away.

After a pause Wu said, "There must have been many difficulties, Uncle, particularly with all the different governments in Southeast Asia."

"It was our rule," said the old man, "to remain independent in spite of governments that changed all the time. We paid millions in bribes. Occasionally we had to find other ways of quieting our enemies."

Ah, Wu thought, at last. He's indicating he's killed when necessary, or had it done.

"What is necessary under heaven must be attained under heaven," Wu said.

Now, thought the old man, we're getting to the heart of this visit. He clapped his hands once, softly, and a door opened. In a matter of seconds a tray appeared with a different style of dim sum, and more wine. Wu looked at it appreciatively.

"The great journey continues, my nephew," the old man said softly. "We must always be in positions of strength. We Han who live in foreign lands are aware of the passage of time, of the many things we must impart to those who will follow us."

Wu considered. "We would be very receptive, Honored Uncle, but you may live ten thousand years."

The old man cackled suddenly. "And enjoy a flower girl and her jade gate every night."

"Of course," Wu said quickly, and ventured a small smile. "Or receive a tael of silver each day . . . or eliminate an enemy each day."

The old man also smiled, and did not contradict. Wu felt bolder.

"I, myself, have certain needs, Uncle, having nothing to do with flower girls or taels of silver."

A killing, then, thought the old Chinese. An important one.

"This house, and all that is in it, is at your disposal."

Wu leaned forward in a deep bow, causing the chair to creak ominously.

"I am not worthy, but most grateful. My father would be pleased to know that his son has been so accepted by his uncle."

"Please have more dim sum," said the old man, and picked up a dumpling and placed it carefully on his nephew's plate. Wu bowed again, this time with an almost imperceptible bending of his bull-like neck. "And now," the old man continued, "our services are yours."

Wu leaned forward. It was time, he knew. "Honored Uncle, there is someone we must kill here in Bangkok soon, but there are certain circumstances that make it necessary for us to seek help. It may be complicated."

"A political affair?" asked the old Chinese calmly.

"No, honored sir. The elimination of an otherwise unimportant man who himself has murdered a colleague and must be punished, else there will be a lessening of discipline and confidence."

"Ah," said the old man happily. It was just the kind of operation that would require logistics, skills, timing and—most of all—subtlety.

Wu watched his uncle. He saw the creased face break into a slow and dangerous smile. "May I tell you more details, Honored Uncle?"

"I am interested in whatever you care to tell me," the old Chinese said mildly. "Your confidences are safe in this house. And then, favored nephew, we will make sure that your objectives are attained. Simply do not consider failure." The old man's chin came up imperiously. "We do not fail," he said.

THAILAND BROUGHT a whole new set of problems, Casski thought sourly, but at least getting through customs wasn't one of them. The uniformed agents, a division of the Army, gave his things a cursory inspection at Don Muang Airport and waved him past.

In front of him Sue Martin pushed a cart with her smaller bags on it, and a porter trailed her with her larger bags. Even watching her back, Casski could tell she was excited; she'd never been in Bangkok before and she looked forward to working the club, to buying Thai silk, to shopping for the sapphires for which Thailand was justly famous. Apparently she had been able to put aside for the moment the growing antipathy that Casski knew stemmed from the tension they both felt.

He realized he had been damned rough on her in the last few conversations. But she'd had it coming. First she wanted to end the whole thing, because as she kept saying, she worried about his life. Then she wanted to call in reinforcements, as if he hadn't been able to take care of Kopalev. Finally there had been the latest gambit from her, that pseudophilosophical argument that his personal desire for revenge would turn him into a monster, no different from the terrorists. Pretty funny, coming from the daughter of those they had killed, he had said, and then had twisted the knife: don't you care anymore?

Her reaction had startled him. She suddenly showed him a face of implacable hatred. She then called him a bastard, and told him that even if this whole operation were called off, she would continue to search for the killers herself. In a voice shaking with emotion, she said she simply didn't want Casski killed in what she now considered her personal cause. He still had trouble understanding it, and once again she had stalked out, slamming the door in what was by now becoming a routine end to their discussions.

He watched her with the porter, admiring the skills with which she adapted quickly to new places and situations. Today she was wearing slacks and a matching bush jacket, a very tailored one with a belt that tied, all in a soft tan. She looked very—competent, he thought, and then admitted it: she was beautiful. He watched the porter and the cabdriver load her bags, with some difficulty, then watched her slip into the cab. He noticed that she took a quick glance around for him first. He grinned to himself, and got the next cab.

The hotel was one that catered to business travelers; it stood between the business district downtown and the notorious Pat Pong sector, replete with its massage parlors and sex clubs, where Japanese and West Germans ended up after charter flights to Thailand especially arranged for lonely bachelors. The streets of Pat Pong were full of people trying to get you into the clubs, trying to sell you hash, hemp, bhang, pot and, once in a while, raw opium from the Golden Triangle. Knife fights were routine in the alleys of Pat Pong, but the real damage was done by the occasional disaffected Army enlisted man who would roll grenades into a massage parlor. Neon signs in the area were gaudy and tended to be references to some facet of Western culture: the White Christmas Massage Parlor, the Rule Britannia Club.

The problems in Thailand, Casski thought, lay in the character of the country itself. He had been here before and found it fascinating, not only for its history and its culture, but for its hustle, and the willingness of people to handle things through unofficial channels. The Thai people were steeped in a tradition of individuality, and while they owed allegiance to King Bhumibol and his lovely Queen Sirikit, they were not awed by most government officials, not afraid of the police, not averse to settling quarrels among themselves without involving the authorities. Casski knew that in the up-country villages the men still carried guns stuck in the waistbands of their pants, and they didn't care who knew it. There were still obscure and remote villages here whose leaders held their positions because they had the best weapons in town. To this fierce independence you could add the influences of climate—incredible heat and humidity broken by driving, monsoon rains—and geography. Because of the country's size and location, just about anybody who wanted to dominate Southeast Asia had to reckon with Thailand, yet it had never been a colony of any other power.

Casski thought abstractedly of these things as he watched Sue check in to the hotel, then went through the process himself. With the advance arrangements he had made they would have a suite, each with complete privacy, but with easy access to the other in case of emergency. Casski followed the bellboy up, tipped him and stood in the center of the room, assessing his next move. It was taken out of his hands by a knock on the door separating his rooms from the girl's. He walked over and opened it.

She stood there holding a bottle of Cold Duck and a plate of cheese. "Compliments of the management," she said, a little stiffly. "Will you help me with it?"

"Sure," he said. She handed him the bottle and walked to the couch and put the cheese tray on a low table. He watched her out of the corner of his eye as he found a corkscrew on top of the suite's small refrigerator and opened the wine. She seemed nervous all of a sudden.

He poured the wine and sat on the couch near the cheese. She came and sat near him but on the edge of her seat, not facing him directly.

"Cheers," he said.

"Cheers." But she did not hold up her glass.

"What is it, Sue?"

She stood up suddenly, put her glass on an end table and began to walk around the room, hugging her arms. He could see the frown of concentration on her face, and a hint of determination. Whatever this was wouldn't be easy for her.

"This is really silly," she said.

He waited.

"Cass…I need to work something out, to talk to you. I just don't know how to start."

He waited, watching her.

"You aren't an awful lot of help."

"Drink a little wine. It might help."

She walked back, picked up the glass and sipped. Her eyes looked smoky. "I need to talk to you," she said.

"Yes, you mentioned that," he said, grinning.

"Damn it, Cass! Help me."

He carefully put his glass down. "All right," he said. "You're getting tired of all this and frightened, and in spite of the way you felt about your parents you want to call it off and go home."

She looked at him angrily. "You know that isn't it."

He looked down, not wanting to see the vulnerability in her eyes. "I know," he said. "I was trying to give you an out."

"It's you," she said.

"Sue..."

"You're the problem, Cass."

She stopped and stood quite still, watching him. He got up and walked with deliberation away from her to stand beside the largest of the room's windows. He looked through the gauzy drapery into the street below.

"I don't want to hear it, Sue."

"Why not?"

"You know why not."

"I'm going to say it anyway, Cass. We have to work this out."

"There's nothing to work out."

"There may be."

He wheeled around. "There can't be, dammit. I'm older than you, I've got a job to do.... There's too much—"

"Not that much older," she said, "and I'm doing the same job. Why are you fighting this?"

Why, indeed? She stood before him, beautiful and desirable. And she could be right. He had sensed that attraction once or twice and realized it accounted for some of the tension between them. Something he wanted to deny. Something . . .

She walked over and stood very near him. He kept his voice as neutral as he could. "In other circumstances . . ." he began.

"Now," she said. "We are living here and now. This is the life we have now. I don't know about tomorrow. I want to know how you feel about me, whether what I'm feeling is silly or not, what to do about it."

He looked at her steadily. "I guess the thing to do is . . . wait."

"For what?" she demanded, not hiding the edginess in her voice.

"Until this is over."

"Are you telling me that you feel it, too? That perhaps—"

"Listen to me," he interrupted. "Just listen for a minute." He paused, gathering his thoughts.

"I don't like working with others," he said roughly. "I've always worked by myself. I like it that way. I didn't know about you when I took this job. In the time we've been together we've had enough arguments, but that's to be expected. I didn't think you would be so . . . uh . . . dammit!" Casski moved back to the couch and picked up the wine and tasted it. "This is no business for amateurs. We've no guarantees. You're a distraction, Sue, and I can't afford that."

He watched her face, the glint in her eyes. She couldn't decide whether to be angry or flattered, he thought. To his surprise she started to grin, then began to laugh, and he found himself grinning along with her.

"Well, Mr. Richard Casski, you're not exactly a silver-tongued devil, but I get the message all right," she said. "Just be aware that we will settle this at some point, whether you like it or not. And meanwhile I'll try not to distract you."

"A deal," he said.

But then all at once she was wearing a serious expression. "Don't play around with me, Cass. If you don't like me, say so. If there's a chance this can grow, say so. And then I'll leave you alone until it's finished."

He looked down into the deep red of the wine.

"Say something," she whispered. "Please."

Something in her voice was an echo of Xixian Martin, and all at once he was back in the water off Repulse Bay, and the water was red with blood, lighter than the wine in his glass, and there were strange popping sounds made by the gun, and the stench of blood and gasoline and the heat of the flames, and unbearable pain. There were the assassins. They would always be there, until he killed them all, and then he would go home and put the gun in a drawer and turn his attention to other things, and killing would be something other people did. But first, the job he had to do, finding them and killing them, and nothing, *nothing* could sway him from that.

He felt her withdraw. He held his breath and heard the pounding of his heart as she moved away. He might never get her back. But first, the assassins. It was a risk.

He heard her close the door, without slamming it. Not angry, this time, but badly hurt.

He turned and carefully set the wineglass down, to demonstrate his own control. He wanted to smash it against the wall. He looked at his hands—steady as a rock. A real professional, he thought. I wonder if, after all this time, I wonder if I peeled away the professionalism, would there by anything left? What the hell does she see in me, anyway? Most of our conversations have ended in fights.

"Christ," he said aloud. Then he picked up his keys and walked out into the streets of Bangkok.

He felt better almost immediately. The street scenes tuned his senses, and as he turned up Surawongsee Road he began to lose himself in his surroundings, tasting the life of the city. The heat and the humidity had his shirt stuck to his back in a matter of minutes, and he envied the Thais in their short-sleeved shirts, sans jackets. His jacket hid the .38 that he now carried everywhere. He picked his sunglasses out of his jacket pocket and put them on and eased through the crowds.

He liked Asia. He felt at home, not at all like what the Thais would call a *farang*, a foreigner. He felt about the peoples of Asia as he did about anyone else; they were not strange to him, or different. He knew the Asian populace as well as any other, and he knew a few Asians intimately. He had realized long ago that aspirations and ambitions, loves and fears, were the same anywhere. In Asia they sometimes revealed themselves in convoluted ways, but they were there, all the same. As he threaded his way through the streets part of his mind remained alert to his surroundings, and part of it mused on the years he had spent in the Orient—some regrets, a lot of gratitude.

He saw a silk shop, with angled glass in the window, coming up. From habit he stopped and looked in the window, the sunglasses hiding the movement of his eyes to the adjacent glass panel that was mirroring the street behind him. He studied it for as long as it seemed reasonable, then pushed off again; nothing on the street bothered him.

An hour later he was in another part of the city, still moving at a fairly fast pace, but absorbing it all—taking in the smells, the sounds, the little vignettes that his mind photographed as part of the texture of the city itself. Most of the *klongs* were gone now, converted into streets, and where once he used to catch the water taxis, now there were buses and cabs. The temples were still there, though, the imposing *wats* with their tall stupas and their gilded Buddhas and the temple lions guarding the gates—fierce carved figures destined to ward off the evil spirits.

He began to feel hungry. He turned into a side street and found a small restaurant. As he went in a young Thai hurried forward, pressing his palms together and saying *"sawadi,"* and then in broken English starting to tell Casski that the restaurant had no food familiar to foreigners. Casski shook his head and smiled, and sat down. The Thai disappeared and came back quickly with a glass of water and a menu. Casski shook his head and

simply ordered *"satay,"* and then, *"Masman
curry. . . kratisod."* He pushed the water glass aside and
ordered a Singha beer. In a little while he was deep into
the meal, enjoying it hugely, and working on a second
beer.

He was reaching for his glass when he felt a small but
perceptible itching at the back of his neck. In a second
his mind translated the sensation: something wrong. A
split-second later the process was complete, and his
brain signaled: someone watching. Without missing a
beat he finished reached for his glass, picked it up, took
a swallow of beer. As he put the glass down he looked
around the small restaurant at the four or five other patrons, all Thais and none showing interest in him. He
leaned back in his seat, merely a foreigner stretching and
digesting a meal. In leaning back he had a view of the
street and the movement on it. Nothing there. And then
across the street he saw the frail body of a Chinese
woman, not young. She was looking down the street,
apparently uninterested in the restaurant or anyone in
it. But Casski thought he had seen her before, a half hour
earlier, in a pedicab.

He finished the meal, put enough baht on the table to
cover it, rose, stretched and made for the door. As he
stepped outside, the woman's glance swept over him and
she walked away, back down the street. Casski turned
in the other direction and moved unhurriedly, stopping
now and then to look into a shop window. A hundred
yards or so from the restaurant he saw the woman's pedicab driver, on foot this time and without the conical hat

he had been wearing. The man had changed clothes and was walking at an angle to Casski from another street. Casski stopped and looked at his watch. The pedicab driver, a lean man and tall for a Thai, walked past him without a glance.

A big operation, Casski thought. They're able to put a large team in the field, multiple surveillance teams with overlapping area assignments. Their mistake is in assuming all *farangs* tend not to notice individual Asians. A kind of reverse prejudice and arrogance.

If they were watching him, they were watching Sue.

Well, that was what this was all about, wasn't it?

He pushed on down the street, thinking suddenly of wily old Sun Tzu. The ideas of Sun Tzu were recently popular in the West, but serious students of warfare had known of him for generations. He was a Chinese strategist who lived probably some four hundred years before Christ, and his advice on conducting warfare was a mixture of patient deception and rock-hard common sense. He could discourse on the use of spies one moment, and in the next advise a general simply to "fight downhill."

So, Casski thought, a little touch of Sun Tzu. "All war is based on deception," Casski remembered. The lure . . . and the ambush. He began to look for a proper site.

He turned into an alley full of shadows from the afternoon sun. It was still a crowded street, but he sensed he was moving away from the heart of town, and in the distance he could see a small stand of trees. He made for them, and as he got closer he could see the stream, a brown, turbid trickle of water with high grass on each bank. Downstream he could see two small boys fishing, and not far upstream two young Thai men were sitting, holding hands. He looked at the sun. Two hours, he thought. In two hours the sun will be blocked by buildings, and it will be relatively dark here. And the Thais will be home, eating early as most Thais do, before going out again in the late evening.

Casski stretched, pretending to be just an indolent foreign tourist. He looked around casually, noting the park on the other side of the stream, the buildings behind him, the other small trees downstream that might provide cover, the openness of the upstream area. He sat down and leaned against one of the trees, pretended to doze.

With his head down he could see the shadow of the tree lengthening. Once, he stirred and glanced at his watch and closed his eyes again. An hour had passed. A little later he stirred again. It was quiet; there were fewer people about now, and even the park seemed almost deserted. Casski put his head back and yawned. The two Thai men were gone and a young man and woman, apparently young lovers, were sitting in their place. But he didn't like the hard look of the man, nor the stiff way they were sitting, as if waiting for a signal. Casski made slits of his eyes and watched them for any movement. Two hours had passed and the shadows were getting longer.

Suddenly the girl got up and smoothed out her dress, and sat back down. Casski noticed she had moved back a little so that now the young man was directly in front of him. He could feel the tension between them, a forced calm. She's given him a field of fire, he thought. But they wouldn't rely on that alone. There would be another one, from behind him.

He sat very still.

The girl seemed nervous and the man said something to her in a low, angry voice. He still had not looked at Casski.

The lure...and the ambush. The man glanced his way. Casski leaped to his feet, took three running steps and jumped the stream.

He landed in the grass and rolled, jerking the .38 out of his waistband, then rolled again in the grass, finally ending flat, with the gun in front of him steadied by his elbows, his body forming a tripod.

Across the stream they were still caught by surprise— the hard young man and the girl frozen, staring at him. To the left of the tree, behind where he had been sitting, another man turned and broke into a run away from the scene, keeping the tree between himself and Casski. Casski had a quick impression of a stocky Oriental man in dark trousers and a white shirt—the garb of literally thousands of Thai men.

He swung the gun back to cover the man and the girl. The man had recovered and was beginning to move—he pushed the girl in one direction and yelled at her, a quick, sharp bark. She began to run awkwardly away from him. The man started in the other direction when Casski shouted.

The man turned and stared as Casski got up.

"That's smart," Casski said. "You can't outrun a bullet. Now stand very still." He jumped the stream again and approached the Thai. As he neared him, Casski saw a look of triumph in the man's eyes—triumph, or defiance. Casski was within ten feet of him before he noticed the man's jaw working, almost imperceptibly.

"Damn," Casski said disgustedly, and leaped for the Thai.

The man had swallowed. His eyes rolled and he went limp. Before Casski could touch him he dropped like some injured, flapping bird. Casski went down beside him, threw him over on his stomach and started lifting him in the middle. It was useless. He turned the Thai over and looked down at the face, still hard in death. The eyes were open and sightless. Casski glanced around— no one close by, a few people on the other edge of the park. He went through the man's pockets, but except for a few baht he was a cipher. There was no identification, no wallet, nothing with any writing on it.

Under the man's loose shirt Casski found a small .22 automatic. He simply hadn't had time to get to it, Casski thought; he must have been holding the poison in his mouth. Casski could see marks where the Thai had filed the serial number from the top of the weapon. No matter; the numbers could be etched out again. But what was the point? They wouldn't be able to trace it in a hundred years. He threw the gun into the stream. Then he stood and slipped the .38 back into his waistband, adjusted his jacket and walked away.

It was getting late, the sun all but hidden. When it went, he knew, it would disappear with that startling suddenness he had seen so often; there were few lingering twilights in Asia. He walked unhurriedly back up the alley he had taken earlier and emerged onto a main street. The traffic was incredible, not merely for the crowding, but for the speed that made the nonchalance of the pedestrians even more surprising. He got a cab whose driver said, "Okay, okay," and shot them out into the stream of cars and pedicabs and buses. By the time Casski was paying the driver in front of the hotel, the lights of the city were flickering on.

He went up to the suite and knocked on the door. There was no answer. He banged it hard, but got no response. He went over to the telephone and called down to the front desk. Had they seen Miss Martin recently? he asked. Yes, said the Thai clerk, in reasonably good English. Miss Martin had left some time ago. She was with a young man, a foreigner. No, he did not know where they were going; she had not asked for help from the concierge nor any of the staff. She had left no message for Casski.

SHE HAD CLOSED the door to the suite and sat on the edge of the bed, dry-eyed and staring into space. After a long time she began to try to think it through. Casski might be right, she thought. They did have a job to do, and she desperately wanted it done. He might not believe it, but she wanted those killers as much as he did; she just didn't want him to die in the process.

As for how she felt, that was harder to sort out. What was the word she was looking for? Ah, yes: propinquity. It might have happened simply because they were together so much. Maybe what she felt was just a mild attraction, magnified because of the circumstances. Maybe if they were in some routine situation, some normal situation, there would be no feelings for him at all. Still, he was fascinating. Hard as a rock. Filled with the assignment to the point where nothing else mattered as much. Had he cared that much for her parents? There must be something he hadn't told her; she'd work on that. She liked the way he looked, the way he moved. He could stir her simply by looking deep into her eyes, unblinking and uncompromising. Whatever else Casski might be, he was a man.

She moved aimlessly around the suite, finally pouring a glass of wine from the complimentary bar. He felt something, too. She knew it. There had been moments in Tahiti when he was lighthearted and happy with her, and there had been the kind of communication that stems from intelligence and the kind of rapport that stems from respect. It was after she realized that he did, after all, like her, that she began to warm to him. But then the assignment got in the way.

She remembered those moments after he had killed the assassin in her room in Bora Bora. She had been unable to check the tears, the tension, the fears for his safety, the assorted emotions that had caused her to spend long moments in his arms. He had just sat there holding her with the same kind of competence he showed in everything else he did. It was as if he had made a list: check the premises, make a plan, kill the assassin, comfort the girl, go on to the next mission. Except for a small, small moment . . . It was brief but she was sure it was real. He had held her with great tenderness and concern and perhaps something more. It was gone before she could think about it then, but she had thought about it long afterward.

Then had come the telephone call and the trip to Thailand. He was all business now. Perhaps it was being back in Asia. Perhaps— She suddenly realized that the doorbell had been ringing for a few moments. She walked over and looked through the round magnifying lens, and felt her heart leap. She unchained the door, swung it open and looked into a grinning, boyishly handsome face; and the next moment he swung her up and kissed her full on the lips and then was dancing with her through the suite.

Peter Carlton.

And all the years dropped away. "Pete," she said, and "Umm," he said, and kissed her. She pushed away and looked at him. It was as if she had seen him that last night in Hong Kong, and it was now only the next morning. Tall, blond, with laughing blue eyes—he was handsome enough to be a model. He was so all-American there was no mistaking him for anything else. It was not only his looks, but his mannerisms, his habits, his lifestyle, even his thought processes. In Hong Kong it had been very different, and charming.

"You haven't changed at all," she said, smiling up at him.

"Boy, you sure have." He grinned at her, showing perfect teeth. She had never been able to resist that grin. It had cheered her at times when she felt guilty, seeing him against her parents' wishes. It had comforted her the morning after that first night with him in the little hotel in the New Territories, when she had had such feelings of guilt and regret. Later, when there had been a very few other nights like that, she had found a lot of solace in that grin, and in the quiet way he talked with her, bringing her out of her shell, helping the girl evolve into the woman.

"I have?"

"You're . . . you're more beautiful. Something has happened, Sue. You've grown up. It looks good on you."

"Pete," she said affectionately, and kissed him again, lightly on the lips. "Sit down and talk to me. What are you doing here? How did you know I was here?"

"Whoa, ma'am, slow down. Can I have a drink first? Would you like one?"

"The bar's over there. I'm drinking wine."

She watched him. He still moved with a kind of boyish grace. He took in the bar at a glance and poured her more wine and began to fix himself a gin and tonic. She had never seen him do anything awkward. He always seemed in control. She had never seen him despondent, or hesitant.

He came back and handed her the glass and sat down on the couch, patting the cushion beside him. She sat close to him and raised her glass.

"To a happy meeting," she said, smiling.

"Sure," he said, and touched her glass with his.

"It's like a holiday," she said to him. "Like some festive thing. An occasion. You're here, I'm drinking wine in this lovely hotel in this lovely, lovely city. . . ."

"And *you're* lovely."

"Pete," she said. "I've missed you." She meant it.

He crossed his long legs at the ankles and looked down at his drink.

"Well, I was a little shook when you left, Sue. You didn't say goodbye. I just went around one day to see if you wanted to go out to Aberdeen and lunch, and your folks told me you'd gone. To America, they said, and that's about *all* they said. I couldn't get the time of day out of them."

"It's such a long story."

"Well, what the hell happened, Sue? I thought I had some small rights in the case. One moment we were, you know, dammit, *lovers*, and the next you were gone." He grinned at her. "Was it something I said?"

"I'm not sure I want to get back into all that," she said slowly.

"Sue, I need to know. You know how I felt about you. I want to know what happened."

She considered it. She ought to ask Casski.

"They sent me away to school," she said. "I thought at the time it was because of you, but now I know it wasn't. They liked you, I'm sure of that. Maybe they just felt it wasn't time for me to get involved. Oh, let's not talk about it now. I'm having such a good time seeing you again."

He lifted his glass in a mock surrender. "Okay," he said. "Well, tell me about your adventures since. How're your folks?"

She was shocked. "My God, you haven't heard?"

"Heard what?" he said, suddenly serious.

She swallowed. "They were murdered. In Hong Kong."

"Jesus Christ!" He was staring at her, wild-eyed. "When?"

"Soon after I left. A matter of weeks. Why didn't you know about it?"

Carlton set his glass down on the coffee table. She saw his hand was shaking. "I didn't want to tell you this," he said. "I ran away. Just plain ran away. When your folks told me you were gone, I just didn't want to stick around. I remembered your grandmother, tried to phone her once from Europe. She wasn't very helpful, or at least she wouldn't tell me much. She sounded a little...eccentric."

"Ah Po," Sue said. "She *is* a little eccentric. And very Chinese. I'm not surprised she wouldn't talk to you. Sometimes she wouldn't even talk to me."

Carlton reached for his drink again with a hand that still trembled. "I'm awfully, awfully sorry, Sue. Did they catch the murderer?"

"More than one of them. And no, they didn't. Well, not entirely."

"I don't understand."

"Pete, let's not talk about it just now. I just want to be happy to see you."

"Okay, let's be happy. No more for now. I know that seeing you again is just wonderful." He turned to look her full in the face. "I hope we can get to know each other again. I'd like to make up for lost time, Sue—that is, if you haven't got anybody else you're serious about."

She looked into the eager blue eyes, the innocent, youthful face. He's like a surfer, she thought, like some California surfer without a care in the world. She looked into his guileless eyes and smiled.

"Pete," she said, "I couldn't imagine a world without you. But let's take it a step at a time."

"I have to know," he said earnestly. "Is there someone else?"

She thought of Casski. Every time she opened a door he closed it. "No," she said.

He reached out and took her hand. "I'm glad," he said and leaned over and kissed her again. "Listen, let's celebrate a little. When you're ready to tell me I want to hear about your folks, but for now, let's enjoy, huh? Are you hungry? Have you seen the city at all? Let me show you around a little. I've been here for a while."

"Yes, no and yes." Sue smiled. "And then I want to hear all about you. What are you doing here, anyway?"

"Tell you later. Let's hit the road."

The grin was infectious, the eyes laughing. All at once she felt younger, prettier. "Let's do it," she said. "I'll get my purse. Where are we going?"

"Ride around town. Lunch at the Erawan. Boat ride on the Chao Praya." He reached out and touched her cheek lightly. "I hope we have lots of time together," he said.

There was a fleeting thought of Casski; maybe she should leave word for him. Then she remembered his face as she'd pleaded with him for some word, some sign. What did he care, anyway? She put him out of her mind.

From the back of a hotel car Peter showed her Bangkok, from the gold-leaf splendor of the *wats* to the grimy back streets. In a Thai silk emporium she bought heavyweight silk for Ah Po and arranged for it to be mailed to her in Hong Kong. In another shop she managed to talk Peter out of buying her a star sapphire.

Over a late lunch at the Erawan he insisted on expensive champagne, and as they sat in the European-style dining room with its Swiss chalet ambience, she found herself enjoying Peter Carlton very much. She wondered if the old feelings were possible. She wondered about a lot of things these days, she told herself.

"You know what I'm doing," she said to him. "I've no idea what's happened to you. It seems like it's been forever since I've seen you. Peter."

He pushed a prawn around on his plate and put down his knife and fork, picking up his champagne glass and looking into it. For a moment she saw a pensive Peter Carlton.

"I left Hong Kong soon after you did, Sue. I just didn't want to be around anymore, without you. I had a little money from my folks—you remember the money I inherited?—so I just went out and got on a plane. There was nothing to keep me in Hong Kong."

She remembered that before she had met him his parents had died and left him enough money to live on for a while, and that he had kept telling her that one day he had to get a job. For her it had meant that she could telephone him on impulse and the two of them could spend a day together—he wasn't tied to a desk. She had liked that.

"So the plane had to come down somewhere," she prompted.

"Paris," he said. "And the next part you won't believe."

"Try."

"Well...I always wanted to act. I got a bit part in a gangster film they were making in Paris. They needed an authentic American accent for it. I got to play a mobster. When I wasn't being a mobster I doubled as a flunky around the set. It was interesting, and I learned a lot."

She smiled at him. "My friend the actor."

"Well—" he grinned back "—it led to other small parts and I found myself working steady. And I kind of liked it."

"So, will I see you in some starring role?" she asked, enjoying the thought of seeing Peter on-screen.

"Maybe," he said, and she thought there was a small note of pride. "I don't know how it will end, but I've done a lot of work—nothing you'll see here. In Europe, though, I think I could do well. There's a German wunderkind making a film in Russia in a couple of months, and I'm going along. In a pretty good role, too. I get to play the guy who shot Rasputin, pretty prominent in the film. They're giving me a week to learn some basic Russian so I can work with an accent, and a couple of days on a shooting range because I've never handled a gun. Then we all rendezvous in a god-awful place in western Siberia called Pokrovskoye, because that was Rasputin's birthplace and authenticity is the name of the game—except for me and a couple of other foreign actors."

"It sounds exciting. You'll be a famous screen star one day. You've got the looks for it, Pete."

"And you'll be a famous singer. You already are a famous singer!"

"No, not yet. Maybe one day."

"Your picture is all over the front of the Club Coronet. I went there looking for you. That's how I found out where you were staying."

"But how did you know I was in Bangkok?"

"An ad in the *World*. The club is giving you a pretty fair promotion, I guess."

"You still haven't told me why you're in Bangkok."

"I had some time off, and a little money from the films. I went back to Hong Kong for a few days, and then just decided to come here and maybe on to India for a few days before I go back to Europe, and get back to work."

"You went back to Hong Kong . . . just for a visit?"

He reached across the table and took her hand in both of his. She looked down at them. They were strong, tanned hands, sensitive, comforting. She felt his eyes, compelling her to look up.

"For you," he said. "You might as well know it. I went back looking for you." His voice was quiet and strong. "What we had, Sue . . . well, I don't want to lose it. I don't want to lose *you*."

"Pete . . ."

"You don't have to say anything now. I know some time has gone by, and I didn't know if there was anyone else for you. I just know that I had to find out. I had to know if there's a chance for us now, after all this time. I haven't been able to put you out of my mind. I guess you know that."

She felt herself softening to him. His touch had brought back a lot of the old memories. It was easy to be here. He was so gentle, so different from Casski. The thought of Casski's square, stern face and his cold eyes suddenly brought her back to the present.

"What is it?" Peter asked.

"Nothing. It's nothing. Let's enjoy lunch, Pete. No serious talk for a while, all right? And then how about that boat ride?"

HONORED UNCLE WAS furious. Wu could see it in the rigidity of the old man's body, the way he held his head. The face betrayed nothing.

"So," the old gentleman said, "the worthless Thai is dead. The man Casski is back at the hotel, unharmed. In the future we will use only our own in this endeavor. We must concede that it has been bungled."

"There is no harm done, Honored Uncle," Wu ventured. "There is no trace to us. There is time to try again."

"It is well the Thai killed himself as ordered," the old man said. "He would have died much more slowly for his stupidity. There were three of them, if you count the worthless woman companion to the Thai. And only one Casski. Is he a superior person?"

"It would seem so, my uncle. As I have related, he has killed a companion of mine, one who was highly trained and motivated, and possessed much skill." Wu hesitated. "Perhaps," he said slowly, "I should not have burdened you with this affair. Perhaps I should proceed alone and remove this worrisome problem from you."

The old man was stung. He looked coldly at his nephew. "And you, are you a superior person? Can you accomplish what others have not?"

"Honored Uncle—"

"Are you now rejecting my help, you hill of flesh?"

"Please, Uncle—"

"Be quiet."

Wu immediately sat back in the stiff armchair, and waited. The old man was marvelous, he thought, a real mandarin. Wu could only guess at his age, but the white wispy beard spoke of many years, and many triumphs. Wu wondered how many people the old man had ordered killed in his long life. No matter. Honored Uncle had survived to have an enormous family who would inherit enormous wealth, and perpetuate both that wealth and Honored Uncle's name. He would be a much-venerated ancestor.

The old gentleman sipped his tea with a steady hand. Still so much to be done, he thought, so much to teach. But this situation with the man Casski must be brought to a quick conclusion.

"We will simply kill him on the street," the old man said. "I will arrange an assassination, by one who will not expect to survive it himself."

Wu knew what it meant. Casski would be killed anywhere outside his hotel. The killer would be some poverty-stricken and desperate young man whose family would be well taken care of if he died killing Casski.

Wu felt a sudden surge of professional pride. Kopalev must have gotten careless. He, Wu, would not.

"Honored Uncle, it is something I must do myself, for my business reputation." Wu knew it was the only tactic that had any hope of success with the stubborn old man.

The old man sat staring at him with eyes like pieces of onyx.

"Let us do this, Honored Uncle, if I may suggest: have your people isolate him, and then I will kill him personally."

Still the old man sat, staring.

"Honored Uncle, the death of this man is a business arrangement. If I do not complete it personally there will be . . . repercussions. In coming to you for help, I am seeking the family's participation, which might be good for the family in the future. I ask now that you help me to get this man alone somewhere, and let me accomplish the task for which I have been hired, and am being paid."

The old man stirred. One clawlike hand fastened around his teacup and brought it again to his lips without a tremble. He put the cup down and folded his hands in his lap. Why not? he thought.

"It will be done the way you suggest," he said, and accepted Wu's respectful little bow of the head for what it was: gratitude that the old man had bent a little. "I will arrange the time and place, and have the *kwai-loh* there. You kill him then, and let us be done with this."

Wu bowed again.

TUGGING HIS EARLOBE, Anderson listened to Casski on a nonsecure commercial line.

"I don't get it," Casski was saying. "They sent a couple of amateurs to, uh, consummate the deal. One of them caught something going around, and the other just dropped it and left.''

''I see,'' Anderson said slowly. ''What do you think it means?''

''I like to think that because they lost that consignment in Tahiti they're having second thoughts, but I know that isn't true. What do *you* think?''

''I think you'd better stick very close to our property right now.''

''That's another thing. It's away from the office. I'm not going to worry yet, but if it isn't here soon I'll need some help with a search. Do you think I could get it from the shipping office, if necessary? We don't want to lose the merchandise.''

The shipping office was the American Embassy.

''No,'' Anderson said quickly. ''Get back to me in a hurry if the merchandise is overdue.''

''Right,'' Casski said, and rang off.

Anderson sat staring into space for perhaps three or four minutes. Then he picked up the telephone and dialed another number in Bangkok.

Time, he thought, to find out what Honored Uncle was planning.

SIX

THE RAINS CAME to Thailand with a vengeance, hard monsoon rains that dropped like a gray curtain. In the jungles the heavy drops crashed into broad green leaves and set up a sound like a waterfall. In the dust of the country roads the rain turned the wheel tracks of the carts into mud, the paths into quagmires. The *klongs* swelled and river traffic was up, particularly along the massive, snaking Mekong, which separates Thailand from Laos. The rain hammered the villages, pounding into the thatched roofs, banging on the corrugated coverings of sheds. It sent rivulets down the unpaved streets and played havoc with attempts to hold the open market sales of produce. But the rains brought smiles of relief to the up-country farmers, whose hardscrabble acres were tough enough to manage at the best of times, and became dry and cracked during the occasional droughts, forcing the girls of the family into Bangkok, where the best-paying jobs were in the massage parlors.

The rains swept in from the northeast, drumming into the courtyard of the Temple of Dawn and onto the spires of the Temple of the Reclining Buddha and hundreds of smaller *wats*. It swept over the palace grounds, over the pleasure domes of Pat Pong Road and into the business district. In the city the rains were merely a nuisance; in the refugee camps along the border of Cambodia the rains provided much-needed water, but also threatened the very existence of some of the bamboo hutches that housed the pitiful remnants of men, women and children who had fled from the excesses of the Khmer Rouge, and later from the domination of the hated Vietnamese.

Casski looked at the rain from the window of a train going northeast from Bangkok. It wasn't an express but Casski didn't care; there was no hurry, and he was seeing countryside he had not seen in several years. The train had taken him first north to Sara Buri, then east toward Khorat. He also didn't mind the rain. He was impervious to weather, a bad-weather animal who could function no matter what the climate. He tried to remember which species hunted in the rain; not many, but he was one animal who did.

And, he had to admit, it was a relief to be away from Sue Martin and her boyfriend for a few days. Anderson had arranged a cordon around them that even he, Casski, couldn't fault. She had round-the-clock protection and somehow, deep in the place where his instincts lay, Casski felt there would not be an immediate attempt. If it came, he had confidence in the CIA types on loan for the situation. It left him free to respond to the signals he had been getting about Wu Kwai-sen.

"He's up there in one of those damned no-name villages north of Khorat," Anderson had said. "We've had two different sightings. He's not exactly keeping his presence a secret. We don't know who or what he's got with him."

"It's a trap," Casski had said.

"Course it is," Anderson grunted in reply.

"I'll just go up and spring it," Casski said. "Can you provide some cover for a few days?"

"Field hands out of the embassy," Anderson agreed. "Already in the works, with an answer for you soon." An hour later the security was in place and Casski felt a momentary sense of relief. I'll worry about it later, he thought. Best thing I can do now is go deal with Wu.

Anderson had called back. "Let's not forget what we're dealing with here," he had warned, his voice crackling in the thin connection with Washington. "We're trying to eliminate a terrorist cell, not start World War III. Try to keep the local talent out of the show if possible."

"How did you find out where Wu is holed up?" Casski had asked.

"Ve haff vays," Anderson replied. "All I can give you is the location of the village. After that you're on your own. I don't want a huge problem there that the embassy types will have to sweep up after." Casski could imagine Anderson sitting there, pulling on his earlobe and scowling. He's trying to bring himself to say they'll have to disavow me if this became a balls-up, Casski thought. "Don't sweat it," he said.

It had been harder to tell Sue Martin he'd be gone for a few days, simply because she was no fool. To her "But why?" he had had no convincing answer. "A lead," he said. "Bearing on one of the terrorists, maybe we can track him down somewhere."

"Then I'm coming with you."

"No, you're not."

"Dammit, Casski!"

"Listen," he said, and on impulse he reached out and took both her hands as they sat on the couch in her room. "First of all, you have the contract at Club Coronet. You've only been there two nights, but they love you. Stay with it. And you've got some good protection here now; these boys are pros, and they'll take care of you. And, of course, there's your friend Carlton."

She looked at him steadily. "You don't like him, do you?"

"I don't feel one way or the other," Casski said truthfully. "At the moment I'm glad he's here—another body to help keep an eye on you until I get back."

"How soon?"

"Three or four days, at the most."

He could see shadows in her eyes. "I'm frightened for you, Cass."

"Please," he said. "Don't worry. Just take care of yourself."

When he started to rise she held on to his hands. "I'll be worried until you're back here."

He could feel her eyes on him as he left the room. Well, he told himself, maybe young Carlton could keep her from thinking about it too much. He certainly seemed to have a way with her. But with his looks and style, he probably had a way with just about any woman he wanted. For Sue's sake, Casski wished he could warm up to the boy just a little. After the reception I gave him, he thought, it's a wonder the kid will speak to me at all.

He had stayed up that night waiting in the dark in Sue's room for her to return. He had simply picked the lock of the door that separated their rooms, and went in. Every instinct he had, told him she was all right; every bit of conditioning told him not to take chances.... If she didn't show by midnight he was going to round up all available forces and look for her.

Sitting there in the darkness, he thought about her many moods. There was the overriding factor that she wanted to avenge her parents' death every bit as much as he did. He had yet to tell her that he had been there when it happened, that it was a miracle he had lived through it himself. Another facet that had surprised him was her willingness to call off the operation because she was afraid for him. And then there was the bit about what it might do to him psychologically, make him into a killer. Casski grinned. He *was* a killer, and it caused him no problems at all. The terrorists who had killed the Martins were vermin who had killed others for the most spurious of reasons. When Kopalev attacked Sue in Bora Bora Casski had hoped to take him alive, but when that became impossible because of the man's skill, he had killed him with an unmistakable satisfaction.

But, he asked himself, what about when it's over?

Back to the ranch, the big sky, the space and the simplicity. And she had a cabin somewhere; she'd mentioned it once.

Could there be more?

Then he had heard the elevator at the end of the hall, and walked over to stand by the door. He took out the .38 and waited.

In a few moments the door had swung open and a shaft of light blazed into the room. Sue stepped in, and behind her a tall figure. Casski moved then, grabbing the person by the wrist and throwing him over one outstretched leg. At the same time he shoved the door and heard it slam. In the darkness he was sitting on the back of the figure with the .38 at the base of the skull. It had happened in no more than two seconds, and left Sue frozen.

"Turn on the light, Sue," he had said quietly. A moment later the suite was filled with light. He looked at the figure beneath him, and waited.

"Cass," Sue had said, fighting for normalcy, "it's all right. This is Pete. Peter Carlton. He's the boy I told you about, the one I thought I was sent away from by my parents."

When he stood up the young man turned and looked up at him. Casski saw a handsome man with friendly blue eyes and an engaging grin. Casski was astonished that the man was smiling at him.

"You must be Casski," he said, and getting up he put out his hand. "A pleasure to meet you. Sue's told me you're a good friend."

Casski swung around to Sue. "Where the hell have you been?"

She started to flare. Carlton stepped in. "Just a minute—"

"Shut up, Carlton," Casski said in a quiet voice.

"I saw no harm in getting out for a while," Sue said. She was starting to lose her temper. "Getting away from you, if you want to know the truth. And Pete here—"

"How much does he know?" Casski had interrupted.

"Not the whole story."

"Then tell him," Casski said, much to her surprise. "If he's going to hang around you, he might as well be useful."

"Tell me what?" Carlton said, a look of puzzlement on his boyish face.

Casski stuck the .38 back in his waistband. "She's got a little story for you, sonny, if you want to hear it. Then, at some point, you and I will talk."

Carlton looked at Sue, an inquisitive glance. He straightened his jacket and tie and turned to Casski, the grin still in place. "I'd appreciate it if you didn't call me sonny," he said, without even a hint of malice.

Casski searched his eyes, found them innocent and unwavering. "All right. You do me a favor. You don't take her places that are dangerous, you don't expose her to the seamier side of this city, you back off when I tell you to, and when you're with her you stay damned close. If at any time I tell you to do something, you do it without question."

"Okay," Carlton said easily. "But if I decide to argue with you, what then?"

"You'll be on the next plane out, and don't think I can't arrange it."

"Okay, Casski. You know I've got her best interests at heart . . . I won't be a problem."

Now, on the train leaving Khorat, Casski admitted grudgingly to himself that the kid was right—he wasn't a problem. He was, in fact, an asset. There was no denying his feelings for Sue. During most of her off-duty time he tagged after her. If nothing else he'd make it more complicated for any assassin.

The assassins. Kopalev dead, Wu waiting for him. Casski felt a strange calm. There was Ahmed out there somewhere; for Casski's money Ahmed was the real menace. He must have conceived and executed the killing of Roget, in Paris. Wu couldn't have done it without attracting hell's own end of attention, and Kopalev was more the bludgeon than the rapier—he would have gone in with a hatchet and gotten both Roget and his mistress. Michaelson's murder in Jakarta could have been the work of any one of them. Morella's in Tahiti was obviously Kopalev's handiwork, lacking all the subtlety that Ahmed might have brought to it.

How to deal with Wu? A mountain of a man, wu shu training, experience. Find him as soon as possible. Kill him fast.

Casski felt the train slow. Out the window he could see the platform, and beyond it a collection of huts, sheds and dirty concrete one-story buildings. He could smell the place, even on the train.

He swung down from the train and walked across the wooden platform. The rain was letting up, but the sky stayed dark and ominous. He loosened the belt of his trench coat and moved briskly toward the center of the village, trying to skirt the muddier parts of the unpaved street. There were very few people out, the rain having driven them indoors. Casski began to look for the kind of place to be found in every Thai village, and in a few minutes he found it—a concrete structure with a corrugated roof that sagged with the force of repeated rainstorms, and in the center, stacks of beer and soft drinks surrounding three or four coolers powered by a small, smelly generator. In the center of this emporium stood the owner, a middle-aged Thai with rapacious eyes, wearing khaki shorts and a dirty white shirt. He had assessed Casski by the time the *farang* had set foot inside the shed, and felt a certain sense of unease. Not your usual tourist, he decided.

Casski stepped inside the shed. A few villagers had collected and stood nearby, out of the rain and watching him. The owner's wary eyes never left Casski as he leaned on the nearest stack of crates and asked conversationally, ''Anyone here speak English?''

There was no reply. Casski hadn't expected one immediately.

He reached in his pocket, pulled out a handful of baht and placed it on top of the stack. ''Anyone here speak English?''

The owner moved then, leaning over to cover the baht with his hand, but not picking it up. His eyes never wavered from Casski's.

"I speak little English," he said in a low voice.

"I am looking for someone," Casski said, louder than necessary. In the silence that followed, nobody moved.

Casski put another pile of baht on the stack. This time the owner leaned over and put his other hand on it.

"No *farangs* in village," the owner said.

"Good," Casski said. "I'm not looking for a *farang*." He turned slightly so that his voice would carry. "I am looking for a Chinese man. He is a big man, bigger than me." He turned back to the owner. "It is business," he said. "Have you seen such a man?"

The owner's eyes shifted then, and came back to rest on Casski. "No see," he said, and Casski knew he was lying.

"Is there a place to stay in the village?"

The owner nodded, and pointed down the street. "Stay there," he said. "Got rooms on top of clothes seller."

Casski nodded and stepped out into the street, feeling the eyes on him. The rain was picking up again and the street was deserted except for a couple of pathetic dogs who watched him, incuriously. Halfway down the street he saw the town's lone clothing store, and turned in.

A young woman sat in the dimness. Around her, in bins, were articles of clothing of the type he saw all over Thailand. The unpainted walls were bare except for a huge portrait of the king and queen, a poster he also had seen all over Thailand. The girl looked up as he entered. Pretty, he thought, like a lot of the country girls. When she smiled and stood up he felt at ease with her, and she said something in halting French that he didn't hear clearly. When he hesitated she spoke in English.

"Hello. I am Vilay. Do you want something?"

"Hello, Vilay," he said, smiling. "I am Casski. I want to rent a room upstairs, and to congratulate you on your English. A mission school?"

"Oh, yes," she said.

"Do you have a room, for a night or two? I can pay in advance."

"Oh, yes, of course," she said. "Do you like to see?"

He nodded, and she turned and led him to stairs in a far corner of the store. She gestured and he followed her up the narrow staircase. She stopped in a small hallway and he counted three doors.

"You may choose," she said.

He paid her the equivalent of twelve American dollars and threw in a tip, which confused her. When she had gone back downstairs he looked around the room: small, dirty, the standard Thai bathroom of a toilet and a sluice pan instead of running water; a functional shower, a low table and a naked light hanging from the center of the ceiling. He could hear the rain on the roof above him, harder now. He sat on the edge of the thin pallet on a wooden frame, and considered: Wu would find him; where did he want to be found?

He went back downstairs, passing Vilay, who was sitting in the same position. She smiled as he passed and he returned the smile, and stepped out into the street again. He turned up the collar of the trench coat, aimed for the less muddy parts of the street and began to walk.

A typical up-country village, he thought. Nothing unusual. There were the bicycle shops, the market square, the food-sellers' stalls. It was too poor a village to boast its own whorehouse. He could smell it, taste it, that odor of a poor Asian village.

He turned and went back to one of the small cafés and went inside, where a wizened old Thai woman watched him, half-fascinated, half-frightened. He pointed to a quart-sized beer in a pan of cool water, and she opened it hurriedly. He looked on the stove, where food was cooking. He could identify some of the dishes, but settled for fried rice, pointing to it and handing over some baht. The old woman nodded, made change for him and fanned the charcoal fire in the stove. In a few minutes he was drinking the beer, warm, and eating the rice, tasty. Long ago he had given up worrying about the lack of sanitation in such places; if you didn't drink the water you could make it all right, even if the food scrambled your insides now and then. And the rice was good.

He took his time over the meal, and when he stepped out into the street again the rain was coming in sheets, driven by a rising wind out of the northeast. He put his hands deep in the pockets of the trench coat and started back toward the center of the village, walking in a growing darkness.

He reached the store and turned in, pausing inside the doorway. The door was open but Vilay was nowhere in sight. He could barely see across the room now. He went over to the stairs and looked up. He took out the .38 and climbed the stairs, very quietly.

At the top he paused again, then started checking all the doors. The tiny thread from the sewn pocket of his trench coat was still in place at the first door . . . and the second. He squatted and looked at his own door. The threads were undisturbed. He stepped into the darkening room. His wristwatch indicated 1830. He sat on the bed, leaning against the wall, the .38 beside him. He waited.

It was less than half an hour later that he heard the first, faint call. He sat up, listening hard in the darkness.

It came again, a cross between a call and a sob. It was a woman's voice, calling his name. It was coming from behind the store.

He went into the bathroom and stepped up on the toilet. Through the open eaves between the wall and roof he looked down. The opening restricted his vision, but he caught the glint of a lantern on the mud of the street. He noticed the rain had stopped.

"Casski," the cry came again, a broken, fluted call like an animal in pain. And then he heard, quite clearly, the hiss of a whip, heard it crack, heard the sudden sharp intake of breath and the quick moan. There was a low, masculine growl, and the girl called again.

He turned and went down the stairs and out the front door, holding the .38 loosely, with his arms at his sides, feeling cold and calm. He rounded the store and walked to the back and stopped.

She stood in front of him, naked in the light of the lantern. He could see clearly the bruises on her face and the caked blood at one corner of her mouth. There was a look on her face he would always remember, a mixture of pain and resignation.

When he looked closer he could see blood running down one arm and trickling onto her hand. But what held his eye was the rope around her neck, leading off into the edge of the lantern's circle of light. From somewhere beyond the circle a deep, soft voice reached him.

"Throw the gun to one side, or I will shoot her now."

Her eyes widened, and appealed to him.

He tossed the .38 to the right, hearing it fall into the mud of the street.

"Vilay," he said.

The rope jerked and she went backward and down in the mud.

Casski stood very still.

"Get up," the voice ordered.

Casski watched as Vilay got to her feet. The rope tightened and she stepped backward, half a step at a time. She stood, not trying to cover her nakedness, head down, waiting.

Into the circle of light stepped the biggest man Casski had ever seen, and all at once the years dropped away. He had last seen this man from the water of Repulse Bay. It was Wu who had poured the gasoline in the water.

Wu was holding a gun in his left hand, his right continuing to tighten the rope. A thin leather whip was pushed through his belt. He pulled Vilay back against him, holding the gun to her temple now and dropping the rope. He reached around with his other hand to caress her. He ran his hand over her breasts; Casski could see her wince. The hand moved down to her pubic hair, and Wu suddenly clutched her.

In the scream that followed Casski moved involuntarily, then caught himself. He had nearly killed her. Wu had come within a millisecond of pulling the trigger.

"Casski," Wu said, and smiled. "Did you kill Kopalev? Alone?"

"Yes," Casski said.

"I'm going to kill *you*, Casski."

"Are you going to hide behind a girl while you do it?" Casski asked, trying to think, trying to stall.

Wu gestured contemptuously at Vilay. "This? This is just the bait. You are coming with me, Casski. I am going to kill you in a most honorable fashion. Pass by me, to the right. I will follow you. If you make a sudden move this one dies. If it does not matter to you, then I will kill her quickly. And then I will kill you."

Casski moved then, grateful for some break, his mind working furiously. Behind him he could hear Vilay stumbling after him, and Wu's footsteps in the mud.

He walked straight ahead, past the last house of the village and onto a path between two paddies. Beyond the paddies was a stand of trees. When he reached them he heard Wu growl again, and he stepped between two trees.

They were in a circle of trees. A perfect arena, Casski thought. Wu had picked his killing ground well.

"Now," Wu said, and Casski turned to face him.

Wu pulled the whip from his belt and threw it to one side. He kept the gun on Vilay as he reached up and untied the rope around her neck. Then he pushed her backward onto the muddy ground, and knelt over her. He began feeling between her legs.

"Another time," he said. "Another time we will see if you have the capacity for Wu Kwai-sen. Now you listen. I am going to kill this *farang*. It is a business matter. You will leave here and say nothing of this night. If you do, I have friends who will know. They will kill you and your family in the slowest way possible. Do you understand! Only your silence will buy your life."

Vilay looked up. Casski could see the terror in her eyes. She nodded.

"Then go," Wu said, and stepped back.

She got up and took one faltering step. All at once she seemed conscious of her nakedness, and tried to cover herself. As she turned, Casski could see the ugly marks across her back where the whip had torn into her flesh.

She turned and threw one glance at Casski. She was asking his forgiveness.

"It's all right, Vilay," he said. "Do as he says."

Both men watched her stagger through the tree line and back down the path.

Casski turned to face the assassin. Wu was at least fifteen feet away, too far to jump. Casski considered breaking for the tree line, finding refuge in the darkness. He wondered briefly about the caliber of Wu's gun, about its stopping power. He heard Wu laugh.

"You are beaten, Casski."

"Maybe."

"But you will not die easily."

In the lantern light Casski watched the huge Chinese move to the right, into a clump of bushes at the foot of a tree. Wu knelt down. When he straightened he was holding something in his hand.

"Have you ever seen one of these?" Wu asked, almost casually.

Casski stared. It was an iron whip, lengths of iron linked by iron rings. Wu held its weight as easily as if it were a nylon rope.

"An old Chinese device, Casski. It's called a *Kau Sin Ke*, a chain whip." Wu's face split into a huge grin. "I'm going to kill you with it."

Casski stood, staring. Then he looked straight into Wu's glittering eyes. "You couldn't kill a gnat, you fat son of a Wan Chai whore," he said, and turned his head to spit contemptuously.

Wu's grin disappeared. Still holding the chain, he raised the gun toward the sky, and with his thumb moved the revolver's cylinder to one side. He shook it and the cartridges fell into the mud at his feet. He threw the gun to one side and raised the iron whip.

Casski was already moving. He feinted to the right and went left, even as Wu began to swing the whip. He heard it whistle overhead as he aimed a kick at Wu's groin. The big Chinese turned the kick aside with his leg, almost as an afterthought, and the whip whistled again.

Close, Casski thought. I've got to get inside.

He felt Wu check the whip's swing and redirect it, an incredible feat of strength. The whip came down at an angle and Casski had to jump back. When he did the whip flashed again, and he felt it graze his elbow, a sensation like being kicked by a mule. For the next few seconds he felt the numbness in his left arm, and he danced to Wu's right, forcing a backhand swing.

This time the whip slapped at his trench coat and Casski, thinking hard, jumped back and dropped his right arm, grasping it with his left. Wu paused, laughed and came at him again.

Casski pivoted and kicked, felt his foot strike home. He heard Wu grunt and step back, flowing into a classic wu shu stance. Casski moved again, staying in motion, the arm dangling. Wu shifted his weight and swung the chain whip again and Casski felt the wind of it within inches of his head.

Wu took the bait—or so Casski thought. The big Chinese feinted as if he were going to Casski's right, then turned swiftly and caught Casski's backward kick and spun him off balance. Casski hit and rolled, his mouth suddenly full of mud. He heard the chain whip thud into the mud beside him and rolled again, lashing out with his feet.

Then he was up again, and Wu had stepped back, grinning. Casski backpedaled, watching Wu's eyes. With the next thrust Wu had dropped the arm holding the whip and had chopped him across the shoulder, a blow that would have killed him if it had hit his neck, where it was aimed. Casski felt the shock of it right down to his groin.

Wu closed again, coming from the right. Casski suddenly pivoted and swung backhand at Wu's throat. He felt the contact, saw the big Chinese stagger, and he leaped inside for a lethal blow to the nose or throat.

He didn't see the whip coming, nor did Wu intend a counterstrike. As he flailed backward the whip came up and caught Casski full in the chest.

Casski went down like a felled ox, feeling a numbness radiate outward from his chest through his whole body. He seemed to have lost control of his arms and legs. He summoned all the strength he had, and saw his arms barely move. And much, much too slowly.

He looked up. Wu had recovered and was standing over him. Casski tried to kick, a feat that was beyond him.

Wu raised the whip. Casski made one last grinding effort to move. As the chain whip went up Wu began a howl of triumph and murder.

A greater noise drowned Wu's cry. Casski heard it roar in his ear. He saw Wu pause. A second raw, banging noise seemed amplified in the night, and Wu looked puzzled, his eyes on something beyond Casski.

With a huge effort Casski rolled to one side and fought to get up. As he staggered to his feet he heard, over the sound of the noise, an impact like someone striking a tree. He saw, then, the hole appear in Wu's chest.

The big Chinese was standing very still. Casski blinked at him and heard the fourth explosion, and jerked his head around.

She was still naked, and her eyes were flat and cold. She held Casski's muddied .38 in front of her with both hands, trying to keep it from wavering. As he watched she fired the fifth round.

Wu staggered. A giant fist unclasped the chain whip and it fell into the mud. He tried to turn his head but his eyes were glazing over. Casski stepped closer and spoke into Wu's ear. "You lose," he said.

Wu pitched forward and lay still. For a long moment Casski stood staring at him, conscious of the soft moaning sounds coming from Vilay. She had lowered the pistol and was standing very still. Somewhere, far beyond the tree line, he heard the rain beginning again, and a quickening wind caused the lantern to flicker, throwing shadows that danced within the perimeter of the trees.

HE LED HER out of the trees and back to the village. It was as if she were in a trance.

There were no lights; the villagers were too frightened to come out of their houses, but he was certain they were peering into the dark, rain-drenched night. He guided her through the front of the store and kicked the door shut. He led her up the stairs and at the top he took the .38 away from her and slipped it into his pocket.

She leaned into him then and let go, her body shaking, her face on his chest. He took her into the room and turned on the light, his eyes shocked by the sudden brilliance. He nudged her gently into the bathroom and held her, careful not to touch her back, while she vomited noisily into the toilet. He sluiced it down. Then he undressed and pulled her with him into the shower and washed them both, feeling her wince as the water ran across her back. With the single thin towel he patted her dry and helped her to lie facedown on the bed.

He went downstairs and rummaged around until he found what he was looking for—a squat jar of green, viscous salve that even the poorest of Thais seemed to have on hand. Back upstairs he rubbed it gently into the wounds of her back. Then he lay down beside her and held her until she stopped shaking. An hour passed. He got up and turned off the light and lay down beside her again. He could hear the hammering of the rain, much stronger now, and he pulled the dingy cotton sheet over them.

He slept for an hour or so, waking only when he heard her stir.

She put her lips close to his face; he could feel her warm breath on his cheek.

"Casski," she said. He lay still, listening.

She moved her hand over him. "Casski."

"Are you all right?" he asked softly.

"If I not lie on my back. Casski, listen," and there was a note of urgency. "Please." He knew that urgency for what it was, a need to reaffirm life.

In the dark room, in the rain-battered night, on the thin pallet, he took her with great tenderness and care, and no little passion. Afterward he thought that of all the other things mixed in with it—the relief, the human contact, the celebration of living—there was also a certain fine and unmistakable joy.

SEVEN

AN ODD FEELING, Sue thought.

She had gotten so used to having Casski nearby that when he wasn't there, he left a void. She mustn't feel this way, she told herself.

She heard the announcer finish, heard the piano introduction and the rising applause. She stepped out onto the stage of the Club Coronet for her first set of the evening, bowed to her accompanist and turned to face the audience.

Through the smoke and the undercurrent of conversation, across the noise of ice in glasses and the voices of the cocktail waitress, Sue felt the familiar rapport with the audience that she had established in the few nights she'd been there. She knew that many of the people were repeat customers, and the club's manager, a narrow-chested Thai with enormous thick glasses and aspirations to be a big-time manager, had told her that business had never been so good.

She had gone into off-the-shoulder gowns because the temperature tended to rise in the club despite the air conditioning, especially when it was filled, as it had been in recent evenings. She stood in a soft spotlight, wearing a gown that was a happy medium between showing her figure and overt sexuality. Her voice, she felt, had never been better.

The audience was mixed, a few Thais, a few Chinese, a few Americans and a contingent of sailors from some Australian vessel. The Aussies made the management nervous, for they were known to be uninhibited when it came to dismantling someone else's property in the heat of battle.

For the moment the audience was relatively quiet. She opened with an up-tempo from a Broadway musical, a song that allowed her to use her range to great advantage. Halfway through it she sensed that it was going well, but she picked up a restive air in the audience, sensing it with a fine-tuned instinct for her audiences. As she moved into the closing bars she assessed the crowd and thought they might be a little older, as a group, than some she had sung to. When the first number ended she signaled a change in the programming to the accompanist. He nodded and led her into a slow, sad ballad that had been popular a dozen years before, and she knew instantly she was right.

The applause rocked the house, and she moved on to a medley of old love songs, an unabashed nostalgic tribute to a slower and perhaps more gracious time. Not a sound now, no coughs, no tinkle of ice in glasses. Even the jaded cocktail waitresses had paused, listening. In the silence of the room she rounded the notes and offered them, pure and true, to the audience.

She had been standing almost motionless behind the microphone. Now she reached for it and lifted it clear of the stand, and began to push it gradually away and above her, tilting her chin and letting the last notes flow gently through the microphone. She closed her eyes, hearing the song end as she wanted it to end, and started to smile.

There was a noise in her ear like a thunderclap and she felt, simultaneously, the microphone jerk from her hand and her arms and shoulders swept by a swarm of needles. Her eyes flew open but the next moment something struck her, hard, and she went down, with a weight on top of her.

"Lie still," someone yelled.

Her heart was hammering and she could feel it, *hear* it above the bedlam in the room. She moved her head slightly to breathe better, and from flat on the floor she looked across the stage to the audience, now in total panic. Everyone seemed to be trying to get to the exits, but she noticed that the Aussie sailors had formed a circle, facing outward, and she caught a glimpse of Prasad, the manager, crawling across the stage toward her.

"Peter," she said, and got no reaction. "Pete!" she shouted.

The weight above her stirred. "Lie still," he said again.

"What happened?"

"Later," he said. "Stay down."

She looked back to see Prasad within inches of her face. She caught a wave of garlic and saw the light glinting from his thick glasses.

"Ah, Miss Martin," he said. "Very sorry."

She began to laugh, feeling it rise and unable to contain it. Prasad looked at her unbelievingly. "No hysterical, Miss Martin!" he shouted. "Please!" She put her head back and howled at the sight of Prasad.

She felt Peter stir and then the weight was gone. She sat up to find him kneeling beside her, his eyes sweeping the room. Prasad had jumped from the stage and was moving through the room, trying to restore order. She looked down and saw that her right shoulder and part of her right forearm were covered with tiny scratches. She looked up at Peter, who reached out and drew her closer.

"It's all right, Sue. No harm done."

"What happened?" she asked, and suddenly began to grow angry. "What happened?"

"Somebody tried to kill you," Peter said softly. In his blue eyes she could read his deep concern.

"We thought that wouldn't happen here, in the club," she said to no one in particular. She felt a deep, cold fury, and in the next instant was analyzing the emotion without meaning to. This is a little bit of what Casski feels, she thought.

"I wish Casski were here," she said.

"I'm here, Sue," Peter reminded her. "You're all right. I'll take care of you. We need to get those scratches looked at. Thank God they're only scratches."

"From what?" she asked.

"The microphone," Peter said. "Somebody shot at you and hit the microphone. It's pieces of it that cut you up. Come on." He began to ease her offstage.

Only then did she think to ask, "Did they catch whoever did it?"

"No," Peter said gently. "But we're all right now. Whoever did it is gone. There's police outside. And," he said with a grin, "there's me and Prasad inside—as good as the Royal Canadian Mounted. Let's go."

In the small dressing room someone poured a brandy. She was conscious of people milling about, and she held on to Peter's arm. He had one hand over hers and in the middle of the confusion she felt his comforting presence. As she sipped the brandy she watched Prasad trying to deal with a squat, ugly police sergeant while others swarmed around the hallway and in the club. She looked at her hand holding the brandy glass; it was steady. The anger that she had felt earlier was still there, and she began to see that it could have its uses.

IT WAS AT KHORAT that Casski first noticed the tag on him; he thought the tall, lean man now shadowing him must have boarded the train there. It would have been easy enough to press in with the crowd.

In any case the man was in plain sight, sitting a couple of rows ahead, a standard technique for allaying the target's fears. People didn't expect a tag to get in front of them. But Casski figured that if he moved, the man would shift his position.

At the next stop Casski waited until the local started up again, then he rose quickly and moved back to the rear of the coach and stepped down. He waited until the next coach was rolling by and swung back up on it. He looked out to see the lean man look frantically around the platform, then jump back onto the passing coach. Casski grinned; the shadow looked disgusted with himself, as well he should be.

The tag came down the aisle of the coach. He was wearing a tropical-weight suit, cut full for such a lean man, and Casski looked for the hint of a bulge under his left arm. A Berns-Martin holster, probably, holding a Beretta or a Llama. The man decided to bluff it out and started to move around Casski, who was still standing in the aisle. Casski crowded him ever so slightly.

"What do you want?" Casski asked softly.

The lean man turned. "You, Casski. I would have contacted you soon."

"Well?"

"Let's sit," he said. Casski studied him, a man with no distinguishing features. Casski was sure he'd cut all the labels out of his clothing, and had erased all telltale characteristics from his face, as well. "I've got a message for you," he said.

"I'm listening," Casski said.

"It's the shipping office. Our clerk wants to go over some invoices with you."

Casski stared.

"So. . . you're going with me to the office?"

"We're doing some remodeling in the receiving room, so the clerk will see you in the annex."

Christ, Casski thought, a real balls-up, and in a fraction of a second he felt a chill. "It isn't Sue Martin, is it?"

"I've been instructed just to bring you along, that's all."

Casski leaned over and smiled. "Answer the question, chum, or you won't be able to stand when this train stops again."

The tag stared at him, then looked down. "It isn't anything to do with the Martin girl."

"Is she all right?"

"As far as I know."

"Good," Casski said. "Now we can be friends." The man looked at him curiously. "Wake me up in Bangkok," Casski said, and put his head back and slept soundly.

The slowing of the train woke him instead, and in minutes they were into the kinetic life of Bangkok. He followed his shadow off the train and into a waiting Toyota sedan and Casski watched the familiar streets roll by. The shadow was silent, preoccupied, and Casski sat back and tried to unravel the mystery. The shipping office was the embassy, the clerk was the ambassador himself, and the annex was the ambassador's residence. If this was so serious that it couldn't take place within the embassy, it was damned serious. He wondered where Sue was now. He wondered if Carlton was with her.

The sedan moved away from the core of the city and out into an area where the streets were wider and there was considerably less traffic. The streets were lined with trees and behind them were high fences with gates guarded by Thai police. Most of the embassies were in this area, and most of the diplomatic residences, as well—a little enclave that housed the Americans, the British, the Indians, the Russians, even the Vietnamese.

The car turned into a driveway and a Thai guard came over and peered inside. He looked at the identification proffered by Casski's shadow, and looked again to make sure he was under no duress. He waved them inside. The car wound around an enormous tree and stopped under a porte cochere. Casski got out and looked up at the house, a huge, white, rambling structure. His shadow waved him inside and he stepped through the door into a cavernous room filled with Thai objets d'art and blocky furniture.

A short, stocky man with thinning hair and a strong chin came forward. Casski had never met the ambassador but recognized him from photos. A former labor leader and a political appointee, he had fooled all the pundits who had predicted his failure; he was greatly admired by the Thais, showed a facility for the language and a willingness to listen. A great quality, John Martin had once said to Casski. Being able to really listen is more important than a lot of things you could name. Except that Martin himself hadn't listened that well.

The ambassador shook Casski's hand with a grip that told of his steelworker origins. He tilted his head and gave Casski an appraising look.

"I'm told you're about equal to a company of Marines," the ambassador growled.

Casski grinned. "You an ex-Marine, Mr. Ambassador?"

"That's right. Fifth Marines, Chosin Reservoir, Uijonbu. Well, what the hell. Somebody here wants to talk to you, and it sounds goddamned serious to me. So see him but leave me out of it; there are things I ain't supposed to know about."

"Yessir," Casski said. He followed the ambassador into a smaller room, leaving the tag behind.

"Here he is," the ambassador said, and abruptly left the room.

Casski stood facing a tall man, so thin as to appear almost emaciated. He was a man in his late sixties, Casski thought. Ivy League to judge by the clothing. The man was smoking a pipe with an aromatic tobacco, and when he spoke Casski immediately identified the upperclass Southern accent.

"I'm David Sinclair," the tall man said, and offered his hand. "It's so good to meet you at last."

Casski shook hands. "Sinclair? National Security Council?"

The man nodded. "That's right. Won't you sit down, Mr. Casski?"

Sinclair arranged himself on a settee, looking as if he might have purchased the house at one time or another. Casski admired the style, the gentlemanly, Virginia blueblood, Scots-Irish, tweedy approach that lulled you into a position where your throat could be cut. He had seen it before.

"What's this all about?" Casski asked, deliberately brusque.

Sinclair nodded and puffed on the pipe, as if Casski had asked an eminently reasonable question.

"I think we have a problem," Sinclair said, in much the same tone he might have used to mention the traffic or the humidity. Casski sat in silence, waiting to see how Sinclair set about unfolding whatever it was that was bothering him.

"You see, Casski," Sinclair mused, dropping the *mister*, "the nature of the business we're in lends itself to deception. After a while it's hard to tell what is deceit and what is real."

"And by extension, who is deceitful and who is not," Casski said.

Sinclair favored him with a broad smile. "You are no fool," he said. "Perhaps you could take it another step?"

"I would say," Casski said slowly, "the real difficulty would be to *choose* between deceit and reality, not in pragmatic terms but in philosophic terms. Deciding what you *want* to believe."

"Ah, Casski, you live up to your reputation."

"What's this all about?" Casski asked bluntly.

"Well," said Sinclair, "I don't know everything, but I sure am scared about what I do know. Let me recap it briefly.

"We have Operation Longbow, which I know you know all about. It's accepted that the Longbow panel is using you to smoke out the terrorists. I know right down to the money how much you've been able to tell the Martin girl, how much you want to hold back. And you're right: it's choosing between deceit and reality."

Sinclair leaned forward. "What do you do when they become inseparable, Casski?"

"How about a for-instance?" Casski said, and waited while Sinclair fussed with lighting the pipe again. Casski was conscious of the coolness of the house, the ceiling fans, the aroma of Sinclair's tobacco, the shadow waiting just outside and beyond him the guard. He thought he knew then how a caged bird might feel, providing the cage was large and airy. And he was growing a little impatient.

"Well," said Sinclair, puffing heartily to get the pipe going, "the Martin girl thinks all this activity is to get the people who killed her parents. We all know better. This, uh, procedure we're embarked upon is a twofold effort, Casski, as I'm sure you are aware. We want to strike at the *Jihadia*, all right, and we want to smoke out the fourth terrorist. And secondly, we want to find the leak in our own organization."

"I'm aware of that," Casski said.

"Well," Sinclair said, drawing the word out, "I think we might have made some progress, but it doesn't make me feel any better."

Casski sat very still.

"When we organized Operation Longbow we had a clear-cut mandate from the President," Sinclair said. "It didn't stop each of the components of Longbow from drawing on its own resources."

I know what that means, Casski thought; they didn't trust one another so they set out on their own little adventures.

"So," Sinclair went on, "my particular group, being the specialists in electronic intelligence—ELINT—well, we set up a lot of little listening posts here and there." Sinclair paused. "We bugged everything in sight."

Casski smiled, a little grimly.

"We picked up a conversation here in Bangkok in the household of Qing Dan—he's one of the old-style mandarins, a real throwback to the warlord days. He moves a lot of muscle in Southeast Asia, when he wants to. We believe there must have been a code worked out in advance, because the conversation was brief. Your name was mentioned."

"What are you trying to say?" asked Casski.

"That there was contact between a member of Operation Longbow and a young woman in the home of old Honored Uncle, Qing Dan. From the transcript it's apparent that it was a one-time code and impossible to break. What's significant is that someone on our board has a working arrangement with someone in the home of that old Chinese manipulator. And that following that call, you were sent up-country, where Wu tried to kill you."

Casski stood. "I can see where this is leading. But you're wrong. I've known Anderson for years. We've worked together."

"He could be a sleeper," Sinclair said calmly, "a mole."

"He could be Little Orphan Annie," said Casski, "but I'd bet he isn't."

"He sent you up-country."

"It's what we hoped he could do," Casski argued. "It's his job to run me where it will do the most good. I'd say he was doing his job, and doing it damned well."

Sinclair also stood, the pipe going and a look of melancholy on his face. "It's very sad, Casski, but I'm afraid that he's become a security risk. Nothing in Longbow's files, or any files for that matter, talks about a contact in Bangkok. You *know* that's the sort of data that must be filed—an occasional, a national at that, that he kept secret? It's against all the rules."

"He doesn't give a shit for the rules," Casski said, "as a rule."

Sinclair pondered this, and looked sharply at Casski. "And you don't, either, is that it? You and Anderson are a couple of adventurers, lone wolves? To hell with the team play? Get the job done in spite of the dreary little bureaucrats?"

"I wouldn't put it quite that way," Casski said.

"But you can't deny it. Well, let me tell you something." Sinclair paused again, his eyes glinting, his voice with an edge of steel in it. "The other members of Operation Longbow no longer trust Anderson. We've now got to figure a way to pull back, cut our losses, get enough evidence to put Anderson away or turn him."

"I don't believe I'm hearing this," Casski said.

The southern gentleman manner was bent but not broken, Casski thought, and the accent was intact. It came through like honey pouring over steel. "It doesn't matter too much anymore what you believe."

"And Anderson?"

"We'll try to turn him, I would think. He's a talent. And he had a formidable reputation. Even the Washington press corps treat him with respect, even though they can't figure out exactly what he does."

Casski turned and stared out the large picture windows at the green sweep of lawn.

Sinclair sensed a turning point. "Take your time," he urged. "You might see the logic in it. You said it yourself—a choice between deceit and reality. It's what they mean by a no-win situation."

Casski watched Sinclair draw on his pipe. The man looked absolutely unflappable, but then he'd had a few days to come to grips with this. Casski stood suddenly, feeling the need to pace. What he also felt was a pulling across his chest, and he couldn't suppress a wince.

"What is it?" Sinclair asked, alarmed.

"I think I have some broken ribs," Casski said. "Wu hit me with a damned chain."

Sinclair stood very still. "Wu? You've done it? Magnificent!"

"In a way," Casski said. "I had a lot of help."

"In a few minutes we'll get the embassy doctor over here and tape those ribs. You'd better get a full physical."

"All right," Casski said. "But what about Anderson?"

"We'll give him enough rope," Sinclair said, the casual charm back in his voice. "If he doesn't hang himself, we will."

"How do you suggest I react to directives from him?" Casski asked, wondering how far the Longbow panel was prepared to go.

"Go along, at least to him. Then you call me. I'll give you a Washington number with a scrambler. Let me know everything he says. Remember this number, Casski," and he gave Casski the number.

"I'd better check in with him," Casski said.

"By all means," Sinclair agreed, tamping down the pipe. "First, rest a little and I'll get the embassy doctor over here. And then I want to hear all about it."

"Maybe not all," Casski said.

THE DARK MAN SAT by himself at a window table, eating toast and drinking black coffee, a morning *Honolulu Advertiser* unread in front of him on the table: part of the tradecraft. To others he was simply another tourist, although a bit exotic. He looked as if he might have Middle East origins, and he certainly looked young and healthy, a tall man with no fat on him, a man with eyes that were quick and intent.

He now turned those eyes on the scene in front of him, beyond the window. Immediately outside was a brief expanse of lawn bordered by a low rock wall; beyond that was an enormous crater, laced by lava flows and here and there sending up white plumes where groundwater met the fantastic heat of the underground magma and turned into steam. On the floor of Kilauea Crater was another vast hole in the earth, the volcanic fire pit the Hawaiians called Halemaumau. The fire pit, he knew from recent but thorough reading, had risen and collapsed a number of times, and was several hundred feet deep.

Between Volcano House, the rustic hotel where he sat at breakfast, and Halemaumau fire pit, were winding trails that snaked through forests and then out onto the crater floor itself. Circling the crater was a fine highway that branched off and ran down a chain of similar craters before plunging down almost four thousand feet to sea level and the boundary of the national park. Along the chain-of-craters road were side roads and trails leading into thick ohia forests graced by darting, colorful birds and a handful of hardy wild goats. And beyond the crater was the Ka'u district, a stretch of near-desert that made the dark man smile to himself, and remember his boyhood in another part of the world. The desolation and bleakness of deserts that so frightened others struck a responsive chord in his soul.

It is a good place, he thought. A good place for what I must do.

He had made the approach with considerable care, because this time the death must seem to be an accident. He had studied the possibilities. Automobile accidents were commonplace, but harder to arrange than anyone believed. There was the sea, but he was a child of the desert. No, the great advantage of this enormous island of Hawaii, called by local residents the Big Island, was its very size and diversity. For the past week he had been driving around, exploring the potential. In its scope and its underpopulation, the island was something special in the Hawaiian archipelago—the youngest and largest in a chain that stretched sixteen hundred miles, northwest to southeast, across the North Pacific. Within its shoreline the island was carved by prevailing winds and weather into definite sections, from a lush rain forest to rolling meadowland, on down to a tropical shore and through the Ka'u desert to the wild, cold, awesome world of the two high volcanoes, Mauna Kea and Mauna Loa, both more than thirteen thousand feet, and the smaller but more active volcano of Kilauea.

It gave him a number of possibilities; the matter of selection was now a matter of taste. He sipped the coffee—only people of the desert could make decent coffee—and glanced back out the window. Here, he thought. I will do it here.

The man whom he now thought of as his quarry came into the dining room of Volcano House and sat at a table nearby, also with a newspaper. Ahmed watched him without seeming to. The target was short, fat and wore thick glasses; a jolly sort with an unlined face. He was the antithesis of all that Ahmed's people had known, a walking refutation of poverty. No, this fat American had never been hungry, never had to kill for food, never had to fight for the rights to water. And because he was soft, he would die. Ahmed would enjoy making it happen, as he had enjoyed the others.

He looked at his newspaper, not reading it. His mind was on the target, whose name was Campbell, and who was a computer expert at the Pentagon. Campbell had a security clearance so high few people even knew its category existed, and because of his access to records and his ability with the computer, he represented a threat. For the past few years he had been working with a sole aim: to correlate all data on the *Jihadia*. Fortunately the movement's highly placed source was able to pinpoint him. His death would leave a void that would take years to fill.

Ahmed decided to make his move.

He picked up the newspaper and moved over to stand beside Campbell's table. "Excuse me," he said, deliberately accenting his excellent English. "I cannot understand some things here, written down. Some part of this story. I wonder if you can explain some words."

Campbell peered up at him. The crucial moment, Ahmed thought. Ahmed smiled gently back at the target. "It is the weather news, you see," Ahmed said.

Campbell put his face close to the newspaper where Ahmed was pointing. "Oh, I see," he said. "Your problem is that isn't an English word. It's Hawaiian. The report says *mauka* showers—that means rain over the mountains. If it drifts *makai* that means the rain's moving toward the sea."

"Ah," said Ahmed, drawing out the word. "You must be very smart."

"Nah," Campbell said, shaking his head. "Just been here in the islands for a few days."

"You have seen much," Ahmed said, making it a statement.

"Yeah, guess so." Campbell squinted up at him. "Where you from?"

"Israel," said Ahmed. "An Israeli and a sabra."

"Sabra?"

"Native born."

"So you must've fought the Egyptians," Campbell said.

Ahmed put on a serious face. "It is no sacrifice to fight for freedom."

Campbell hesitated only a moment. "Sit down, have some coffee. What're you doing here?"

"On leave," said Ahmed easily, sitting down. "I am a major in the Israeli air force. I have convalescent leave, so I travel. This is an interesting place, would you say?"

"Sure would."

Ahmed led the conversation; Campbell was eager to talk. He is a fool, Ahmed thought. In a job like his he should be careful who he talks to. Ahmed had a sudden thought: he may be a homosexual. He may think I am.

In a half hour there was a growing rapport. Ahmed was careful not to inquire too closely about the target's occupation, only enough for it to seem a normal part of the conversation. They talked about the island, the weather, the racial mixture, the coming era of the Pacific so much talked about in the media. Ahmed managed to convey that his funds were limited and that he would have to leave soon. It was, in fact, his last day. Campbell seemed genuinely sorry.

"But tonight," Ahmed said, "I am going to do something I have heard much about."

"What's that?" Campbell asked.

"I will walk down to Halemaumau, to see the fire pit in the moonlight. It is said that the Hawaiian fire goddess, Pele, sometimes shows herself by moonlight."

"Hell," said Campbell instantly, "I'll drive you. That's too far to walk. After dinner you think?"

"Oh, yes," Ahmed said, smiling broadly. "But I like to walk. So... I meet you there, we both look for the goddess. You drive us back!"

"Okay," said Campbell, and after a moment's hesitation, "You want to have dinner together? Here?"

"Ah, I cannot," Ahmed said. The last thing I want is for someone to remember us together late tonight. "But I will meet you at the fire pit tonight. Say eleven o'clock?"

"Say ten o'clock. Everything closes up earlier here. Okay?"

"Okay, my new friend," Ahmed said, smiling, and he shook hands with Campbell. As he left the dining room he saw Campbell signal a waitress. Fat pig.

He spent the rest of the day exploring—on foot, careful not to be seen driving a rental car. He walked down a couple of the trails, hiked through forests of fern, explored an enormous lava tube, an open-ended cave made centuries ago by the force of fast-rushing lava. He walked the bleak trail where falling pumice from Kilauea's flank eruptions had stripped the ohia trees of leaves, leaving them stark, their branches etched against an overcast sky.

At dusk he showered and dressed warmly against the cool air of the four-thousand-foot elevation. He slipped out a side door of the hotel and walked swiftly off in the darkness. He found the paved road easily and began to stride, enjoying the air, the space and the white moon surrounded by a sky of brilliant stars. Long before ten o'clock he was in the vicinity of Halemaumau, but he stayed well away from the fire pit, not wanting to be seen by any late sight-seeing tourists. Finally he walked into the parking lot, from which he could easily make the edge of the fire pit in a ten-minute walk. In the darkness he could see pretty well, thanks to the moon, and he could smell the sulfur from the earth.

He looked at his watch: 2145. If Campbell kept accurate time, he'd be along in fifteen minutes. He sat on the curb of the parking area and waited.

He saw the headlights of the car arcing down the road from the direction of the scientific observatory. He watched as the car took the curve around to the left and headed toward the parking area. He looked away from the lights and waited as the car neared and stopped a few feet away.

Campbell got out, dressed in a hooded jacket and carrying a flashlight.

"Well, Major, by God, we're here. Ain't this some night out here?"

"Wonderful," Ahmed agreed. "Like in Israel, like the Negev with its brilliant stars. You must visit my homeland some day."

"Damned right," said Campbell. "Want to hike on over to the pit?"

Ahmed let Campbell lead the way with the flashlight, although they could see without it. In a few minutes they were at the edge of Halemaumau.

"May I borrow your light?" Ahmed inquired politely.

Campbell turned and handed it to him. "Pretty out here. A little cold. So... we're gonna see a fire goddess, hey? Come out of the pit?"

Ahmed was careful to turn the light off. With an easy motion he lifted his arm and tossed the flashlight into the pit. He heard it hit once and bounce off into the dark.

For a moment Campbell didn't realize what had happened.

"What the hell? You drop it?"

"No," said Ahmed, in clear and unaccented English, "I threw it into the fire pit. A little gift for Pele."

Campbell squinted at him in the darkness. "What's the matter with you?"

"Not a thing, you overstuffed American pig," Ahmed said pleasantly.

"I'm getting out of here," Campbell said, but he found Ahmed blocking him. "Get out of my way," he said, but there was a quaver in his voice.

"Listen to me, Campbell," Ahmed said. "You have been judged by the *Jihadia*, and your crimes are enough to justify your death. Your technology has helped to advance imperialism and to repress the true believers. You are an infidel, and I am going to enjoy killing you."

Campbell bolted, but it was too late. Ahmed seized him by the jacket as he tried to pass and a swift, hard jab to the kidneys put Campbell on the hard ground. He lay there. Ahmed heard him start to sob.

"Ain't done nothing to you," Campbell whined. "Nothing to you."

"Get up," Ahmed said coldly. "I may let you live."

Campbell scrambled to his feet. Ahmed shifted slightly to keep him nearest the fire pit.

"You want to live?" he asked Campbell.

"Yes, oh God, yes." Campbell was almost babbling.

"Renounce your God," Ahmed said quietly.

"What?"

"You must deny your God. You must admit it is all false, that there is no God but Allah and Mohammed is His Prophet."

"Yes, yes," Campbell said. "That's right."

"Now," said Ahmed. "Face Mecca and pray."

"Yes," Campbell said, and Ahmed could see tears on the American's face.

"That way," Ahmed said, pointing.

Campbell got down on his hands and knees, facing across the fire pit.

"What do I say?"

"Say goodbye," Ahmed snarled, and kicked him as hard as he could.

Campbell grunted in pain and pitched forward. He was on the edge of the fire pit, and loose cinder and soil began to slide beneath him. He started to turn over when Ahmed kicked him again.

Campbell went over the side and bounced once, very close to the fire pit's rim. Ahmed heard the scream start and listened to it growing faint, until it stopped.

Ahmed looked up at the sky. A few tendrils of cloud hung about the summit of Mauna Loa, and there was a long, dark streak of clouds far on the horizon to the south. Otherwise, the Hawaiian night was clear and bright and promising, and with a jaunty step Ahmed started back toward the hotel.

"IT HAS ALL THE EARMARKS of our Sudanese friend," Anderson said. The secure line he was using gave his voice a slight Donald Duck quality, the way divers sometimes sounded in talking to the surface. It was totally incongruous with the rawboned Anderson, and it made Casski smile.

"Is Campbell going to be as irreplaceable as you seem to think he is?" Casski asked.

"I don't know," Anderson said. Casski could almost see him pulling at his ear. "I can't talk to these computer people. They never give you a yes or no, just a lot of bullshit about the complexities of what they do. I look at a computer as a glorified adding machine and they think it's artificial intelligence. So I ask them why we call it a computer instead of a thinker. That always pisses them off. Anyway, it was a damned shame about Campbell. We had no idea Ahmed would move so fast on it. We had planned to get Campbell aside when he got back and work out an entrapment with him, but Ahmed reached him first, the son of a bitch."

"You didn't answer the question," Casski pointed out mildly.

"Well, there's always somebody else, isn't there? I grant you it's going to screw things up for a while, but we'll work it out."

"So, tell me where we are now," Casski said carefully.

"Two assassins dead, thanks to you, the third in Hawaii and being watched now. We'll try to keep him under surveillance. As for the leak, we're closing in on that, too, but it's not your concern at this point."

"Why not?"

"Because if we change the game plan we'll spook our man. You just keep after them and we'll do the rest." Anderson paused, and Casski tried to sense his thoughts, to read him over the miles. "Anything bothering you?" Anderson asked abruptly. He was, thought Casski, half in admiration, a man who could sense a subtlety, feel a nuance in the air. It was why he was where he was.

"Nothing's wrong," Casski said. "I just wondered how you were doing there and what the big picture was." He waited.

"Listen, Casski," Anderson said, and Casski thought he detected more warmth in the voice. "You sit tight until I can put you onto Ahmed. When that's concluded we'll know more, because it will bring some people out of the bushes."

"Maybe it has," Casski said, deciding to risk all.

"What do you mean?"

"Sinclair's here. I met with him today."

Anderson let out a yell of pleasure. "Damned good! Good! It's moving. He's bent out of shape, right?"

"Very bent," Casski said.

"Damned good! Now—" Anderson was all business "—the next move is that he'll try to discredit me with Longbow."

"Sinclair's a double?" Casski asked.

"No, no. A damned good patriot. Just mixed up about who the traitor is. He thinks it's me, and he'll see to it that I get more and more isolated from what's going on. What that will do, combined with you putting Ahmed on ice, will both frighten and encourage our sly little friend, whoever he is. I think it might be enough to make him show his hand, so to speak."

"So where is this bastard you're trying to nail? Somebody on the inside, with you, one of the principals?"

"Can't tell you any more, Cass; this has to be played out as naturally as we can make it. Just proceed, and stay in touch. By the way, if you tell me why Sinclair's annoyed it might help me at this end."

Casski hesitated.

"Cass . . . you've got to trust me. I can walk it back, maybe, if you tell me the reason Sinclair's pissed."

"It was a telephone call you made to the home of one Qing Dan."

Anderson grinned; Casski could feel it down the line.

"I've got a lady in that house who talks to me; had her there for years. Honored Uncle would wet his pants if he knew who it was. But what you've told me helps me take it back through our communications net. It gives me a starting point.''

"Listen, Anderson. I don't care much for all this double-and triple-play crap. I want those three men; I've gotten two of them, and if in getting the third I can help you, then that's fine. I have to tell you, though, when Ahmed is in my sights, that's as far as I go with you.''

"We have an agreement," Anderson said quietly. "You wanted the terrorists, right? And I wanted to find out who's working both sides of the fence in this little group. Now I've delivered the terrorists, and when you knock off Ahmed—and don't think that'll be easy—you have to do it in such a way as to bring *my* quarry out where I can see him. At least you have to try.''

Casski grunted noncommittally.

"Cass, you bastard. Listen to me. What if I told you the man I want is the one who *ordered* the other three to hit you and the Martins? That he is, in effect, the fourth assassin? One and the same.''

After a while Casski answered, "I can't trust you that far. You'd say anything to keep me on after I kill Ahmed. Anyway, you haven't told me how you know this, nor why you've waited so long to tell me. We've always worked in terms of three assassins.''

"It's simple enough, Cass. You and the girl have to keep going on a set track, acting naturally, acting out of the very basic motivation you actually have. If you start playing games it could jeopardize everything, and actually put Sue Martin in greater danger.''

Casski sighed. "I'm too damned tired to argue right now, and my ribs hurt. What's the next move, then?"

"Shift to Hawaii."

"How soon?"

"I want the Martin girl to put in about another two weeks in Bangkok. We'll get something for her in Hawaii, provided Ahmed is still there."

"Where else would he be?"

"He'll be awaiting orders. The next command he gets will be to eliminate you, then the Martin girl. We'll let the entertainment sections of the Honolulu dailies know she's coming—we're already geared up to do that through a friendly on one of the papers—so Ahmed will probably decide just to stick around and let you come to him."

"So for two weeks we just watch her, huh? Good. I need the time to recuperate. Anyway, she'll love it, with all the attention she's getting from Peter Carlton. I suppose you know all about him, too?"

"Yeah. Did I hear a little sliver of jealousy there, Cass? Is this girl getting to you, hey?"

"Up yours, Anderson." He could still hear Anderson laughing as he rang off.

Casski went downstairs in the safe house, a place the embassy people didn't know about out on Withayu Road, not far, he reflected with irony, from the Vietnamese Embassy, down at number 8311. There were other people in the house now—security officers, the housekeepers and a duty officer. Casski ignored them and went into the large living area. Behind the bamboo bar he found the ice chest and fished out some ice and dumped it into a glass, then filled it with the finest whisky he had ever tasted—Caol Ila, a single malt from the island of Islay, off the Scottish coast. "Scots wha' hae," he said as he sat in a deep rococo chair. He took a long pull and savored the whisky. His ribs were aching.

He thought about the fourth assassin, who had not been present that fateful day off Repulse Bay, but who had caused it all. Casski started to hate him even more than the others. And then he gave way to it—to a deep, clutching, satisfying hatred that transcended everything. Anderson, goddamn him, had known it would grip him this way; Anderson had him in his pocket. It wouldn't be enough for him, now, to kill Ahmed, to have wiped out the three men who murdered the Martins. As long as there was another one—a fourth one—he and Anderson wouldn't be finished with each other. The fourth assassin. Faceless, nameless, crawling around out there in the darkness, in the evil night. More dangerous than the others because more secret. Well, he would get his. But first, Ahmed.

EIGHT

HE AWOKE TO A LIGHT tapping at the door.

"Casski?"

He looked at his watch. A few minutes past 4:00 a.m. He sat up in the darkness and ran his hand underneath the pillow, feeling the .38.

"Come in."

The door opened, and beyond it Casski could see the lighted hallway. He could make out the silhouette of the duty officer, an older man, who had struck Casski as ex-military when they met the day before. Casski wondered how many duty officers ran the house—probably three shifts.

"What is it?" he asked.

"Thought you might want to see this Reuters report," the duty officer said, and in the dim light Casski could see he was holding a sheet of telex paper.

"Thanks," Casski said. "Mind getting the light?"

In the sudden brilliance Casski blinked and took the single sheet of paper, torn from a telex. The dateline was Washington.

In the late afternoon, Washington time, an unknown number of fighter-bombers operating from United States bases in England had conducted a raid on terrorist facilities in Libya. Joined by aircraft from two U.S. carriers in the Gulf of Sidra, the planes had hit targets in Tripoli and Benghazi. There was no damage assessment as yet, no word on Libyan casualties or damages. American casualties were limited to one aircraft down. There had been no strike in Syria. The strike in Libya seemed to have been aimed at specific targets. Khaddafi had escaped injury, but members of his family were reported wounded. Some European countries were condemning the strike, while England was standing firm with the United States.

"We've had no amplifying statement through our own net as yet," the duty officer said, anticipating the question. "I guess they've better things to do right now." Casski heard the wistfulness in his voice: the old campaigner wanting to be at the center of things.

"You've got enough people in the message center?"

"Sure," said the duty officer.

"Keep it coming, will you?" He handed the paper back. The duty officer nodded glumly and left.

Casski got up and showered and shaved. By the time he was dressed there was a second tapping at the door and a fresh-faced young nisei brought him a second report and informed him that breakfast was available, even this early. Casski took the paper and walked out, trailed by the nisei, and went down to the dining room. In splendid solitude he ate an enormous breakfast with several cups of coffee. From time to time the nisei brought him additional scraps of information.

There was every expectation that the raid, whatever else it accomplished, would trigger a new wave of terrorism, a retaliation against the United States and against Americans overseas. Casski speculated that the British would come in for retaliation, as well. He was on his third black coffee when Anderson called the safe house.

"You've heard," he said.

"Tell me what you can," Casski said.

"Well, the French, the Spanish and the Italians refused to let us use their airspace. The F-111s had to dogleg around. There's going to be a lot of diplomatic jinking around in the next few days and weeks. The administration isn't going to let some of these 'friends' of ours off the hook. The Brits were magnificent. Margaret Thatcher is the only head of state with any balls, if you'll pardon the apparent contradiction. I would imagine that in the weeks to come there'll be a lot of cashing in chips. I can believe you'll see a lot of arm-twisting pretty soon, but in the end the allies are going to stand firm . . . and together."

"What about the prospects for more terrorism?"

"Ah, yes. You can look for that. The Brits are gearing up for it—they fully expect it. The Israelis have told us quietly that it was about time we joined the real world, and that retaliation is the only thing that makes any sense. At that, the Israelis feel we didn't go far enough."

"Tough people."

"The world's last realists."

"What does this mean to *us*?"

"I don't know. I don't think Ahmed will get involved. They've got a lot of cannon fodder they can throw into a new wave of indiscriminate bombings and shootings, and that's what they'll do. The cooler heads will decide that knocking *you* off, then getting the girl, will take precedence. So I think we're still on track. Of course, I'm having my problems here."

"How so?"

"Sinclair's been able to convince people that I'm not to be trusted. They're setting up a little entrapment here, and I'm supposed to walk into it. Goddamned amateurs! We're our own worst enemy, sometimes."

"At the risk of sounding like a broken record, what does *that* mean to us?"

"Means you'll reach a point where you have to act on your own. I'm going to try to use this situation to give our sleeper friend a little rope. I'll try to lull him a little, make him think I'm being isolated. In reality, Cass, I'll keep running the show, because there's enough people around who still trust me. I guess, to answer your question, all this means to you is that I might be able to identify the fourth assassin—our security leak in Longbow—and handle it from here. If not, I may be able to give you all I know and trust you to take it from there. If Sinclair—bless his misguided, patriotic heart—is successful in cutting me out entirely, then you're going to have to pick up the ball and run with it."

There was a long pause. Faintly Casski heard Anderson shuffling paper on the other end. "When are

you going to make contact with the Martin girl again?''
Anderson asked abruptly.

"Any time now," he replied. "Probably today. Are
you worried about her?''

"No. She's in good hands."

"I know that," Casski said testily. "You sound like
you know something I don't. We've had embassy people around her all the time, but I'll get on over there very
soon, maybe within the hour. What else does she need?''

"Casski, Casski," Anderson admonished. "Did I say
she needed anything? She's got one of our best men
around her constantly."

"Oh?" said Casski, taken aback. "And who's that?''

"Peter Carlton," said Anderson. "He's one of ours."

In the long silence that followed Casski thought he
could hear a lot of noise on the connection. It was a fan-
tasy he had had as a child, that if you telephoned a long
distance you could hear the elements in between—the
wind blowing over the mountains, the ocean waves, the
desert heat causing the telephone wires to curl and snap.
"Goddamn it, Anderson," he said.

"I couldn't tell you before. I can now. Try to cooperate."

"He's a damned playboy," Casski shouted.

"One of ours," Anderson insisted. "Put aside your
personal feelings. And one other piece of information."

"I can hardly wait," Casski said, with heavy sarcasm.

"Ahmed had a younger brother. He was in a terrorist
training camp in Benghazi when the F-111s hit it. So

now Ahmed is the last of his line, and he knows it. We aren't sure how the word got to him so fast, but he knows his brother was killed. He's going to be even harder to handle, so watch your ass. And be ready to show up in Hawaii in about ten days. We've got everything under way. Anything else?"

"No," said Casski, with feeling. "That's quite enough."

IF IT ISN'T LOVE, thought Sue, I don't know what I'm feeling. And if it is, how can I feel it for two men?

She turned over and looked at the ceiling in the early-morning light. Dammit! There was Casski. Strong and sure. She would never change him, rule him, dictate to him. He would call the shots in any relationship and if she didn't like it she could get off. It had a certain appeal, but it was the kind of appeal a modern woman should shun. Casski was, in the end, an old-fashioned man. Peter, on the other hand, was younger, charmingly vulnerable, a damn sight more *cuddly* than Cass would ever be. Peter had more charm, more sophistication. Peter would be understanding, where Casski would tend to swear. Peter would let her mother him; Casski probably never had a mother, or if he did she was a timber wolf. Peter was twice as handsome, but Casski had a strange kind of attraction. Peter was a fox, Casski a wolf.

How was this going to end? And when?

She got up and parted the curtains. From the window she could see the boat traffic building up on the Chao

Phya. She could see the lunch wagons setting up, the *sam lor* drivers clustering at the end of the street. The myriad birds that crowded all the wiring over the street had returned, with daylight, to the Pat Pong area, and two bright spots of color turned out to be two hookers, making their way home at first light.

For a moment she gave way to wistfulness, thought about her cabin, high and clean up in the snow country, strongly alluring because of its very simplicity. No mean decisions to make there—or would there be? The Chinese side of her, the pragmatic side, surfaced to remind her that whichever man she picked, he might not want her. Especially if it was Casski. He might not want anybody, the damned pigheaded, stubborn, uncaring man.

Peter, of course, was another story, all solicitude and attention. He might smother her, in time. But then he could be... trained. Sue wrinkled her nose. Had she actually thought that? What a bitch she might turn out to be! You don't train people, you accept them for what they are. And yet...

The telephone rang. She moved back and picked up the receiver and spoke into it.

"Sue, listen, sorry to bother you..." Peter's voice ran on cheerfully, exuberantly. She found herself warming, just listening to him. "It's early, I know, but I need to get an answer from you."

"What is it?"

"Well, it's good news and bad news, as they say. First the good news..." The good news was very good indeed. Peter's old friend, now a successful director, was filming in Hong Kong. A kung fu epic of sorts, but there was a part for Peter that would pay him better than anything else had for some time, and he wanted it. The bad news was that it had to be immediate. So he was leaving shortly. "Would you," he asked her, with elaborate casualness, "like to come along?"

She stood still, thinking, assessing.

"I know you haven't been back there since . . ." Peter's voice trailed off. "You have to go back sometime," he said finally.

It was true. And suddenly she wanted to see old Ah Po, her grandmother. She wanted to go back to a city she had once considered home, or at least as much home as she had ever known, until the cabin. She hadn't realized, until this moment, how much she wanted to do that. It would be a kind of release as well, a catharsis.

"I couldn't go for a couple of days," she said hesitantly.

"I know," Peter said. She could hear the cheer in his voice. "Your gig is up this weekend, then you're free. So you'll do it?"

"Well . . ."

"C'mon, Sue," he said. "I know you want to do it. So let's go, hey? It'll be fun."

"All right," she said, making up her mind. "Are you going to handle the arrangements?"

"Sure. Leave Don Muang on Tuesday, okay? Tuesday night we'll be eating chow fun in the little restaurant in Aberdeen. Remember?"

"Yes," she whispered, remembering the last time they were there, and the night that followed. She listened to Peter, still excited and happy. "Yes," she said firmly. "Let's do it. I'll tell Casski, when I see him again." And when will that be? she wondered.

AHMED RENTED A CAR, using the Israeli passport. The international driver's license was still valid. He had taken a taxi to Honolulu International Airport and gotten the car there at a peak period, with several international flights in at once. The harried clerk had hardly glanced at him. They had taken him by shuttle to the car lot, where he picked up the Nissan sedan. He drove it carefully out of the airport complex and eastward back toward Honolulu, catching the last of the town-bound traffic.

He drove leisurely, partly because of the congestion, partly because timing was important. He knew roughly where his rendezvous would be and how long it would take to get there, and he was in no hurry. By the time he was moving through Waikiki the sun had dropped into the sea like a giant orange flower folding, and the stars were out. He put on his headlights and drove on around Diamond Head, past the lighthouse and on out Kahala Avenue, leaving the air conditioning off and the window open, smelling the soft night and the faint odor of flowers and plants.

As he drove he tried to remember the last time he had had a personal meeting with his control, the man known only as Scimitar; it had been several years ago. Scimitar was very careful. Hardly anyone saw his face. He was the most accomplished assassin the Jihad had ever known, and as a result he had emerged as the leader of their little group. He could kill in an infinite number of ways, and he always made sure he had his own escape route. Ahmed had seen him last in Belgrade, where Scimitar had gone out and killed a prominent Slavic writer whose propaganda had become intolerable, and whom the Jihad had marked for death.

Ahmed turned off Kahala and doglegged up to the highway running east through Aina Haina and Kuliouou and Hawaii-Kai, letting the scenery slip by in the dusk, letting the Nissan flow easily with the stream of traffic. He was still early, but then, no harm in waiting at the scene instead of dawdling in the traffic. By the time the traffic was thinning a little around Hanauma Bay the night had dropped darker and a slight wind was coming off the ocean. There were fewer lights now, and the stars were glittering. He began to look for landmarks that had been targeted, and when he finally saw the golf course's clubhouse to his left, he slowed the car and looked for a place to pull off. In a few minutes he had parked and locked the car, and was walking over a rough lava flow toward the line of surf two hundred yards in front of him.

After the first few steps he was glad he had come early; the rough lava—Hawaiians called it *aa*—was hard to walk on with city shoes. On the other hand, it discouraged a lot of traffic, especially at night. There was not likely to be anyone else on the beach, and if there was, it would be a fisherman walking by. Ahmed alternately looked at the breaking surf, to keep his bearings, and at the lava underfoot, to keep from twisting an ankle. Scimitar, a quick voice on the telephone, had described the spot where some lava outcroppings made a small beach within the beach. Ahmed was to wait there.

He found the place easily enough, and glanced at his watch. He was early, but that was all right. He looked up and down the beach and saw no lights, no fishermen. Above the hissing of the wind and the crunching of the breaking waves on the sandy beach, he could hear the distant sound of cars on the highway. Finally he sat and waited.

He thought about his brother. Another score to settle. He could see the scene in the Benghazi camp: the young boys in training, the sense of brotherhood, and then the jets streaking in, silent at first and the bombs coming without warning. In the wake of the bombs would come the high, keening sound of the jets, and with incredible speed they would be back, and the bombs would tear men to pieces.

Ahmed started at a sound behind him.

"Hello, Ahmed," Scimitar said.

Ahmed grinned and looked around. "Well, my leader, my brother. A long time since we've met this way." Scimitar grunted, and Ahmed watched him getting comfortable on the sand beside him.

"In the West," Scimitar began, "they don't care much for what they call small talk, what the men of the deserts think of as good manners before getting down to business."

"In the West," Ahmed said, "all they know how to do is kill."

"I am sorry about your brother, Ahmed."

Ahmed nodded.

"We will avenge him. What you have done already has been of great importance."

"Which?" asked Ahmed.

"The killing of Campbell. He was very close with his computers. I think in a matter of days he would have been able to identify me, and I would lose my ability to know what Longbow is up to. As long as we are privy to that information, we can stay ahead of them. But it's getting more difficult."

"Why is that?"

"There are games within games. Too much to tell you. I will say that we have now reached the point where we must terminate the Martin girl and Casski, as soon as possible. We know the Martin girl will be in Hong Kong shortly. Casski will follow."

"So," Ahmed said, "that is the next assignment?"

"Right."

"I am glad," Ahmed said, with feeling. "The man Casski has been a problem since the day we failed to kill him in Hong Kong, when we terminated the Martins. As for the girl—" Ahmed made a gesture of dismissal. "In the desert, our women know their place."

"And yet you must be careful," Scimitar warned. "Kopalev, I think, was overconfident. Wu simply let a woman get in the way of his job, from what we could learn from the villagers where he died. The targets are proving more difficult than we thought, however you look at it.''

"Please," said Ahmed, his voice cold. "Do not worry about it. I will find them in Hong Kong and both will die."

In the night, Ahmed could *feel* Scimitar thinking.

"There is no other way, of course," Scimitar said. "Meanwhile, I will keep working on Longbow from within. The Americans are notoriously free with information. Also, I have been able to sow some discontent and suspicion among them, so that there is a strong element of distrust. Knowing the American bureaucracy, if we can succeed in dismantling Longbow, it will be some time before the Americans can put together another, similar organization."

"Is it that you are in a position to influence Longbow's activities?" Ahmed asked delicately, knowing Scimitar hated to be questioned.

"You are asking my job within Longbow," Scimitar said softly, "and that is something you cannot know. You know that I function as your control; that there are others of you in the same capacity—some of whom you know—and that my information is always—*always*—accurate. That is all you need to know."

Ahmed sat in silence. The waves seemed to be breaking closer inshore, and he wondered when high tide was. The wind was picking up a little, also.

"The Martin girl," said Scimitar, after a time, "undoubtedly will stay with her grandmother. The old lady lives in a huge house up on the Peak. You won't have any trouble finding it. Casski will probably try to stay there as well, if the old woman will let him. If not, he'll probably stay in one of the larger hotels, simply because they are convenient and close. It would be desirable if their deaths could look accidental, but if that is not possible, do whatever you have to do.''

"I see," Ahmed said. "Is there a timetable?''

"As quickly as it can be managed," Scimitar answered. "Do you need anything?''

"I am running short of funds," Ahmed said.

"After you left your hotel room I slipped in and left a packet of money in a kit in your closet," Scimitar said. "Then I followed you here.''

"You followed me?" asked Ahmed, shocked.

"Yes," said Scimitar. "Don't grow careless, brother.''

"No," Ahmed whispered, still shaken. He sat and thought about it, amazed that he could have been followed. He looked seaward, thinking.

"Scimitar?" he asked quietly. And got no reply. He turned to see the other man, a shadow only, walking back across the lava toward the road.

After a while he, too, walked back across the lava, and later that night, by telephone, he arranged his flight to Hong Kong.

NINE

"IT IS GOOD TO SEE YOU in this house again, Tsu-wei," the old woman said, putting down her tea and tilting her head back a little to look at her granddaughter. "I have been worried about you."

"I'm sorry," Sue said. "I wish you hadn't worried."

"It's the only thing I have left to do," Ah Po said with asperity. "I'm alone in this house except for the thieving servants, damn their eyes, and I'm so rich I don't have to work. What am I supposed to do?"

Sue saw the slow smile begin around her grandmother's lips. She had almost forgotten some of the charming things about Ah Po—her subtle sense of humor, her unflagging devotion to her family, her occasionally salty language, learned in her youth. Sue smiled and studied the older woman.

Ah Po sat in a squared-off rosewood chair of typical Chinese design, part of the furnishings in one of the myriad rooms of the enormous house. The high-ceilinged home was quiet and thickly carpeted, furnished with exquisite taste and stuffed with objets d'art from all over the world. The old lady herself looked like something chiseled from sandstone, a Chinese woman of average size and configuration, but wearing a cheongsam, the high-slit sheath dress seldom seen on the streets of Hong Kong anymore. Ah Po also wore square granny glasses, and often tilted her head back to look through them at anyone within close range. Her eyesight was worsening, she had told Sue, to the point where she no longer drove the Rolls through the crowded Hong Kong streets. A lot of joss sticks were probably burned in gratitude, Sue thought, because she remembered Ah Po's hell-for-leather driving style. And, added Ah Po, Hong Kong was no longer the fun place it used to be. Sue demurred; the city looked and felt the same to her.

"It's the damned Chinese," said Ah Po irritably. "I mean the bastards from Beijing. Do you know about the disaster that's coming in 1997?"

"You mean the reversion of Hong Kong to the government of China? I don't know too much about it."

"I'll tell you about it," the old lady said testily. "The British and American and Chinese taipans took this rock when nobody wanted it, and built it up to be the greatest free port in the world. In 1997 the sons of bitches in Beijing are taking it back.

"Now you can go around town and you hear nothing but confidence. The cocktail party talk is that the People's Republic will leave Hong Kong alone, that the old entrepreneurial spirit will prevail. Anybody who believes that must believe that chickens don't crap. Given enough time they'll turn Hong Kong into the same kind of inefficient, mindless bureaucracy that runs the rest of their country. Damn!"

"Well, we'll see, won't we, Ah Po?" said Sue, mildly.

"We ought to," her grandmother said. "You look healthy enough. Would you like some more tea?"

"Yes," Sue said, and her grandmother rang a little bell, summoning a middle-aged servant who turned up at once and went away with the tea service.

"Enough politics," said Ah Po suddenly. "By 1997 I'll pull *my* money out of here and put it somewhere else. I'll hate to lose the house, though. A lot of memories here..."

"My mother grew up here, mostly," Sue said softly.

"Her room is untouched," the old woman said, also dropping her voice. "I've saved it for you, if you want it. But there's plenty of room here, if you don't want to sleep in it."

"No," said Sue. "I'd like that."

"Your father used to stay here sometimes," Ah Po said. "Even before they were married, when he was courting her. It was very un-Chinese of me, but I let him stay here."

"In separate rooms, of course."

Ah Po grinned. "They had adjoining rooms with a sliding panel that your mother knew about, and didn't know that I also knew about it. My husband had it built. There are rooms and panels like that all over the house. I think he was building in some safeguards. When your father stayed here, your mother and he would look at each other about eight o'clock and start yawning. It was funny to see. In a half hour they were both pleading they were tired. It was all I could do to keep from laughing at them as they went up to the 'separate' rooms. They thought they were fooling us all.''

"You're right," said Sue. "It was very un-Chinese of you.''

"And you, Tsu-wei," asked the old lady gently, "have you come to grips with your divided worlds? You seem very un-Chinese to me much of the time, but you also have the blood, and at times I can see it, not in the way you look, but in the way you think.''

"How, Grandmother?"

Ah Po started to answer, then stopped when the servant returned with the tea. Sue had noticed that her grandmother, too, moved in more than one world. The tea service was silver, in the best English fashion, and Ah Po took her tea with milk, a very un-Chinese action.

"How, Grandmother?" Sue asked again as the servant was leaving.

"You have not mentioned some things," Ah Po said, "although we have talked now for a couple of hours. You are hiding things in the Chinese part of your mind. And because I have a Chinese mind I can tell you what some of them are. First, you had a specific reason to return to Hong Kong at this particular time. Then, there's the fact that you haven't mentioned men—so you must be having problems with them, damn and blast them. Am I right?''

"Well, grandmother, I have to admit . . . that's part of it.''

"Very Chinese to keep some things hidden, child. As for the unimportant things, there's no gossip in the world like your typical Chinese worker-woman. Listen, when I want to know things, I either go to my fortune-teller in Sham Shui Po, or I go down and listen to the Hokklo boat people. That's why I don't believe all the cocktail talk about Hong Kong's future. But never mind. How can I help?''

Suddenly Sue was flooded with emotion. She put her tea down and went over and sat on the floor next to Ah Po's chair, the way she had done when she was a child. She put her head against the old woman's knee, taking comfort from the touch. "Grandmother," she whispered, "I just want to be around you for a while. Later on I'll tell you everything that's happened. Right now I just want to be here, next to you."

She felt her grandmother's hand on her head. "Don't worry," the old woman said. "You're home here, and safe."

Sue felt the tension easing. She hadn't realized how uptight she was until the Thai Airways jet landed at Kai Tak, and the memories came flooding back. She had even resented it when Peter tried to hold her hand and talk to her. The emotional strain had led to their sudden quarrel outside the terminal building, when she insisted on going straight to Ah Po's house and he wanted to see her safely ensconced in the Hotel Peninsula, where he was staying. She put her foot down and hit him with a burst of Chinese invective—she later wondered where she'd learned it. She finished by telling him to go to hell—*she* was going to Ah Po. She had left him standing with his arms akimbo, staring after her as the taxi pulled away.

Ah Po had seemed genuinely happy to see her, and not particularly surprised. Sue thought the old woman had hardly aged, and told her so. She had reached that point, Ah Po replied, where you couldn't get any older and the next step was death, and she wasn't ready for that just yet. And never mind the traditional filial respect, Ah Po had added, and gathered Sue in her arms and made her feel welcome.

She did feel better. She raised her head, and Ah Po moved her hand. Sue smiled up at her grandmother. "I'd like a long warm bath, a cold drink and a quiet dinner with you, Grandmother," she said. "Is that all right?"

"Damned right," said Ah Po. "You go on up to your mother's room and get ready for your bath. I'll get the rest going for you. Ah, Tsu-wei, it's good to have you home."

Sue went up the ornate staircase to the second level. With a hand that trembled slightly she pushed open the door to her mother's room and stepped inside. It was clean and airy, and there were fresh-cut flowers on a table. She had been in this large room many times, and had always liked its tasteful furniture, and its space and the sense of freedom it inspired. She walked into the large bathroom, and began to take off her clothes.

Downstairs, the old lady sat thinking and sipping her tea. Something terrible has happened, she thought. Not as terrible as the death of Tsu-wei's parents, but terrible all the same. She would need to know more, but not from Tsu-wei.

A servant padded up; a telephone call, he said, and she went over to the marble telephone table and lifted the receiver. She waited until she heard the servant replace the receiver in another part of the house, then answered in Chinese.

The voice that replied spoke English, the same voice that had talked with her earlier.

"Is she there?"

"Yes," said Ah Po.

"Good. You know what to do, then?"

"Yes," Ah Po said again, her heart beating faster.

"I've tried to tell you how important it is."

"I understand, dammit. I'm not stupid."

"Sorry."

"Is there a time?" Ah Po asked.

"It could be any time now."

"All right."

She heard the click of the receiver, and put the telephone down gently. *It could be any time now.* She looked across the huge room, thinking of the size of the house and the grounds. For the first time she felt a small ripple of fear.

AHMED HAD TAKEN a room in a small hotel as close to the base of the Peak as he could get. He didn't want a long commute to the grandmother's house while he was armed. To get caught carrying a concealed weapon in Hong Kong was serious. He would be carrying the 9 mm automatic; nothing clever this time, like the slingshot he had used in Paris. He just wanted Casski and the girl in his sights. There would be no escaping, this time.

He got out the map once again. There must be no mistakes. He knew exactly where the house was and how to get into it. Most of the servants would be gone later in the evening. There was nothing, nothing, that could stop him now.

SUE WENT DOWN to dinner in her best cheongsam, looking and feeling totally Chinese. She wore both jade and gold, and she felt beautiful, and clean and rested. The bath had been a marvelous restorative, and when she got out there had been a cool drink waiting on the side table. She felt calm and in control, and she looked forward to a lingering dinner with Ah Po. The house felt comfortable again, the memories were good ones. Here and there she found, or sensed, traces of her mother's presence. Instead of bothering her, they were comforting.

It's partly time, she thought, time passing and the bad memories starting to fade, while the good ones are strong. It's partly being here, where there were so many good times. And, of course, it's Ah Po, hardly changed from years ago, and it's Hong Kong, too, as magical a city as ever existed, a modern Xanadu. She hoped Ah Po was wrong about the changes the Chinese government would make. Well, she thought, there's still time to do a lot of shopping, and she smiled. She was still wearing the smile when she walked into the dining room and saw Peter.

He saw her at the same time, and rushed over. "Don't be angry," he said, talking quickly. "I asked Mrs. Li if she would invite me here tonight. She was very gracious. Please, Sue . . . I just didn't want to be apart from you yet. We aren't out of the woods with this thing, you know."

"Oh, Peter," she said. "It isn't that I don't want to see you. It's just—"

"I know," he interrupted. "I know what you're going through. Don't forget, I know you better than anyone. But listen, just let me stay near you awhile. I know you'll have guards here, if you haven't already. But I want to be here, too. For you. Please, Sue."

"Oh, all right," she said, hearing the slight irritation in her voice. "I can't actually chase you out of my grandmother's house, can I? It's up to Ah Po, really."

"Oh, she's great, a great lady. She says it's no problem. I'm afraid I sort of popped in on her."

Sue looked at Peter's impeccable dinner suit, at his dancing blue eyes and his trim, boyish face. "I'm sure you charmed her," she said, with a hint of irony. "Well. You're here. Let's have dinner."

"A drink first," Ah Po said, coming into the room, trailed by servants. "I'm glad this is all settled."

She led them into a small sitting room off the large dining room. "Let's sit here for a while, hey?" she said. "The damned dining room is like eating in the middle of a cricket field. My husband and I used to eat in here, but for tonight we'll have a drink here and then we'll meet at one end of the table down there."

Peter glanced at the dining room table. It looked as if it would seat forty or so in comfort. "I'm with you, Mrs. Li. This room is comfortable enough."

They sat on deep maroon upholstery while the servants took drink orders. Ah Po asked for a double gin, straight up and damned cold, while Sue preferred a white wine. Peter ordered vodka, then sat back to favor both women with a wide smile. "This is wonderful," he said. "I'm very grateful to you, Mrs. Li."

"What the hell," said Ah Po. She began to tell them about the time she and her husband had first looked at the property, then gone out and mortgaged their only assets to get the money to buy and build. The house had brought them nothing but luck. All the time they lived there, their fortunes just kept rising. Their investments were shrewd and bold and profitable, and her husband became a household word in Hong Kong, one of the great entrepreneurs. He was on the honors list and might have achieved knighthood if cancer hadn't killed him much too soon.

The story launched her into other tales of Hong Kong, and with Peter's encouragement, she talked about earlier and more exciting times. They had a second round of drinks and Ah Po was still reminiscing when she led them into the dining room.

Ah Po's taste in food was not confined to Cantonese cooking. The kung pao scallops were straight from a Schezuan chef. The duck was Northern Chinese style, and the myriad other dishes reflected the enormous variety of Chinese cuisine. Ah Po smiled to see Peter eating with gusto, and to see that Tsu-wei had lost her drawn look and was enjoying herself. Ah Po forced herself to eat, to drink, to keep talking and not to think about the strange man who was waiting upstairs in the dark.

ANDERSON PULLED on his earlobe and looked glumly at the other men in the room. "It's not that we haven't made any progress. We've come a hell of a long way. It's just that by the time we find our man he could be the hell and gone. I don't just want to know who he is, by God, I want to have him hanging here by his testicles."

Sinclair nodded. "I know what you mean. He even had us at each other's throats . . . well, at least me. I'm still sorry about that."

"No problem," Anderson said affably. "We learned from that, just as we learned from poor old Campbell's murder."

"I don't think I quite got that," Admiral Akers confessed.

Anderson looked at him dourly. "I need to spell that out? All right. Campbell was one of our top computer men, a strange little guy, but our security checks kept clearing him. Anyway, some time ago I put Campbell on a search. I came up with a hypothetical traitor in our midst, gave him all the projects that could be or had been blown, even back in the days before Longbow was officially launched. I gave him all the data I had on the top two tiers of management here—us as the controllers, plus the senior-grade field people. I told him to try to match the traitor with one of us.''

"Jesus,'' Akers breathed, "that could take a lot of time.''

"Well, it did,'' Anderson acknowledged. "But toward the end it looked less and less like a hypothetical situation and more and more like there was a sleeper here.''

"That's when I jumped in,'' Sinclair said. "I knew what was happening, but I thought Anderson was sitting on the results—because they led to him. That and a few mysterious telephone calls were enough to put me over the edge.''

"No matter,'' Anderson said, still in a forgiving mood. "You were out there trying, and doing damned well at it. You were so good you almost put a wrinkle in the whole process.''

"Uh,'' ventured the admiral. "Back to Campbell?''

"Sure. Campbell got close enough to the data match-up to scare the bejesus out of the traitor, who decided to eliminate Campbell so we'd have to start over. Not only was Campbell killed but he took a lot of data with him. He'd stored some stuff in his head...too sensitive to put on paper. With Campbell out of the way, we would have to bring somebody else along, covering the same path. Which would slow the whole process...give our sleeper time to get out and cover his tracks.''

"So,'' Sinclair mused, "we did make some progress? I can't see any.''

"We made a very important find," Anderson said. "What we found is that it isn't one of us—that is, not one of us here in this room. The man we want is among our senior field men."

"Christ," said the admiral in an uncharacteristic burst. "That's scores of people . . . well, at least dozens."

"At least dozens," Anderson agreed. "And we're working on it now."

"More time," said Sinclair. "We just need more time."

"That," said Anderson, "is what we haven't got."

THE FIRST GUARD was easy.

Ahmed saw him silhouetted against the night sky when he should have been sitting lower. Ahmed watched, to see what he could learn. Instead of occasionally sweeping the area with night-vision equipment the guard simply sat there. Given a reverse situation, Ahmed would have been lying in deep shadow, using a masked light source and a pair of PAS-5 binoculars, the kind the Israelis used. One day the carelessness of the West would be its undoing. Ahmed unsnapped the dark covering over his watch and looked at the glowing dial. He would give it twenty minutes.

He looked at the house. Guards outside, probably guards inside. Certainly silent alarms, electronic surveillance. At least an independent generator. A staff, plus the old woman. And the girl, his target. Where was Casski? No reports on him for days. No matter.

The house was daunting, but not impossible. He looked at his watch again. Twenty minutes and no rotation of guards. Very careless. A man began to grow lax after a few minutes in the dark; rotation prevented that. Ahmed flexed silently in the dark, alerting the muscles. Then he began to crawl around the guard, watching for wires, watching for danger from any direction.

In the Benghazi training camps he had been the best. No one even came close to his skills, possibly because no one shared his passion and his hatred. Ahmed knew that of all his contemporaries he was the one blessed, and cursed, with imagination, the kind of imagination that allowed him to see what the desert could become, what the depressed and despised people could attain, and how severely the Israeli bastards and their Western allies had oppressed the men of the desert. More than anyone he knew, Ahmed took that oppression personally. He had been robbed of opportunity; the infidels had stolen his future. At the same time they had robbed an entire race of its nationhood, they had degraded one of the oldest religions in the world, and they had made the proud desert tradition into something trivial.

Because of that he had become the killing machine he was, and because of that he had erased all feeling for his victims. He was merciless. Of all the assassins in his group, he was the only one motivated by idealism, and it made him the most dangerous. Except, possibly, he conceded, for Scimitar, whose motivation was never clear to anyone, but whose skills were legendary.

Ahmed stopped, lay still for a moment. It was his habit to indulge in a few minutes of mind play before the final stalk on his target, but now he had done it, now it was time for the machine to take over. He emptied his mind, putting away all thoughts not related directly to the situation at hand. After perhaps a minute and a half, he felt the familiar coolness, the total dedication and the total absorption. Now he could act without thinking, could become the instinctive, reflexive organism that allowed nothing to stop him.

He crawled past the first guard, despising the man for the ease with which he had gotten by him. Now there should be someone else, someone in the shadows of the house. The second guard should have radio contact with a command center inside the house, with specific contact times and authentication codes. Let them play their games. Ahmed had no intention of harming any of them—that would only alert the others. No, he would simply melt into the house, and there he would fire the shots that would forever end the Martin girl's life.

He crawled into a row of bushes beside an easement to the house, a pipe of some sort. It was cool to the touch. In a few moments he had made his way past the house, then doubled back, approaching it from a slightly higher elevation. He stopped and looked at it again. The windows would be too difficult, but some of the older homes here had screens underneath the eaves. He would try the roof, perhaps swing down under an eave. That way he could leave their whole security system in place. He lay studying it. There was a tree relatively close, but it would be a long, noisy jump. The tree was perhaps twenty meters to the right. He began to ease toward it.

"YOU'VE NO IDEA how much Hong Kong gets in your blood," Peter said. "I mean, I wouldn't want to spend all my life here, but it's great to visit."

Sue placed her napkin carefully on the table, still listening to Peter but watching Ah Po out of the corner of her eye. Her grandmother seemed slightly distracted this evening. She was polite enough, even animated, but her speech was somewhat restrained and she seemed to be listening with only half her attention. Peter, obviously, had not noticed.

The dinner had gone well, Sue thought. Peter could charm anybody when he wanted to, and he had set out to make Ah Po like him. The fact that he felt it necessary was curious, she thought, and immediately followed it with another idea: Peter was acting like some suitor, over to talk to the old folks about their daughter's hand. Was he coming on a little too strong?

"You have to live somewhere," Ah Po said to Peter. "If you can travel, what difference does it make? People these days, flying around everywhere . . . we thought coming from Shanghai to here was a big move. Nothing, these days."

"Tell me about Shanghai," Sue said. "Mother was born there, wasn't she?"

"She was," Ah Po said, and her face cracked in a wide, thin smile. "We were among the last to leave after those Beijing bastards took over. Chiang was no prize, but

Mao and that crew...they had no class. Before them, life in Shanghai was...lovely. Lovely." And she began telling them about the days when she was young, and surrounded by family.

Sue listened, fascinated. Ah Po seemed unaware of both her and Peter, talking for herself, playing out the memories aloud as if hearing them was a way of keeping them alive and vibrant.

After a time Sue felt Peter stir slightly, and she interrupted her grandmother. "Let's go into the Dragon Room, Ah Po, and have an after-dinner drink; Peter's getting thirsty."

Peter grinned. "Great idea," he said, "but I hope you'll go on with the stories."

Ah Po rang a small golden bell, and servants appeared. One of them, a small, wizened man, preceded them into a large room next to the dining room, heavily carpeted and decorated with a dragon motif. A large painting of the traditional red dragon, under nonglare glass, dominated the room's objets d'art. Among the several small statuettes of sandstone dragons were some of pure ivory and some of jade. Sue was familiar with the room, and she smiled to see its impact on Peter. He stood, apparently awestruck, while the servant slid open a teak panel and began to put a variety of liqueurs on a silver tray. Sue heard Ah Po hastening the servant out. She would fix the drinks herself, as a courtesy to her guests.

Peter selected a cognac. Ah Po took yet another gin with ice and gave Sue an amaretto. They sat in deep, comfortable chairs, and Peter finally was unable to contain himself. "My gosh," he said to Ah Po, "this is a fabulous room. It's beautiful, impressive."

"Damned right," Ah Po agreed. "My husband used to bring clients in here after dinner, just to let them know..."

Ah Po's voice had trailed off. Sue looked at her anxiously, and at the same time was aware of a sudden tension in Peter. "What is it?" she asked. But her grandmother was staring past her. Sue turned.

A tall, dark man in dark clothing stood in the doorway. In his right hand, dangling casually, was a gun. In that first shocking moment it wasn't the gun that frightened Sue most—it was the coldest, emptiest eyes she had ever seen.

Ah Po was the first to recover. "What do you want?" she said huskily.

The dark man stared at them without expression.

"How did you get in?" Ah Po asked, her voice angrier this time. "I'll have you arrested."

"No," said the stranger. "No, you won't do that. Please introduce yourselves. Now."

Ah Po drew herself up. "I am Mrs. Li and I am the mistress of this house. Who the hell are you?"

The man swung his eyes to Peter.

"I'm a friend," Peter said quietly. "Peter Carlton. If it's money you want, let's go outside and I'll give you my wallet. It's very full. We won't call the police."

The dark man's eyes moved. "And you are Miss Martin. Martin Tsu-wei. I have been looking for you."

Sue forced herself to speak to him. "Are you one of the monsters that killed my parents?" She felt the hatred rising, clutching her chest. Her heart felt like a hammer but her mind was cold and clear.

"You won't get away with this," she said, surprised at the calmness in her voice. "I have friends who will find you and make you pay for this."

"If you mean Casski, he is next on my list."

Sue knew that in the next few seconds she was going to die. It's surprising, she thought, how simple things become. This man will kill me and it will all be over. I wish I could see Casski again.

The man raised the gun and pointed it at Sue, holding it in the classic stance of the dueler.

Sue looked straight into his eyes. She heard Ah Po, moaning involuntarily. From the corner of her eye she saw her grandmother start to move in front of her, protectively.

Two things happened at once: Sue heard a fierce, guttural cry, and the dark man hurtled into the room, the gun flying from his hand.

And there in the doorway stood Casski.

"Evening," he said.

She found her voice. "Casski! What..."

"Wait," he said. He walked over and looked down at Ahmed, amazed at the man's recuperative powers. Casski had assaulted him with a classic tae kwon do leaping kick, striking him squarely in the back of the head, yet here he was, moaning and trying to sit up. Behind him Carlton was moving over to hold Sue, who was still staring at Casski. He saw Ah Po pick up her glass and take a long drink.

Six feet from where Ahmed lay was the gun. Casski picked it up and put it in his jacket pocket. Ahmed was sitting now, his eyes coming back into focus and sweeping the room. Casski looked at him for long moments, remembering.

He heard someone stirring behind him, and Ah Po's voice. "I thought you had waited too long," she said.

"I wanted to make sure," Casski said. "I had to let him come by me. But he's our man, all right. Let me introduce you to Ahmed. His profession is terrorism. His tools are anything lethal. His motivation is a need to kill the enemies of the Jihad. And he's in deep trouble right now, because he's going to tell us much, much more."

"You knew he was coming here tonight," Sue said. She turned to Ah Po. "*You* knew. All through dinner. You knew Casski was in the house."

"Someone had to know what was going on," Ah Po said, with a trace of satisfaction. "Assassins in the house! Better than a kung fu movie." Ah Po began to grin. "And we caught the bastard! He doesn't look like much right now."

"Don't let it fool you," Casski said. "Search him, Carlton."

"Right," Peter said. "Get up, lean against the wall."

Ahmed got slowly to his feet, looking at Peter. "Who are you?"

"One of us," Casski said shortly.

Sue jerked around. "One of *you*?" She swung back to Peter. "Is it true?"

"Yes, it's true."

"Dammit!" Sue said, her voice rising. "I'm just an assignment. To both of you."

"No," Casski said. He tried to remember the poet's line about the possibility of losing something making it valuable, but gave it up. "You're more than that."

"Against the wall, now," Peter said to Ahmed.

Ahmed rolled over and got up gracefully. He spread his legs and leaned against the wall. Peter walked over and began to search him.

Casski glanced back at Sue and her grandmother. "I hope you two are all right," he said. "We still have a few things to do here."

"Don't trouble yourself about us," Ah Po said.

"Casski, is he . . . is he . . . ?"

"Yes," Casski said. "He is. I'll never forget them."

Suddenly, Sue knew. The words tumbled out. "You were there. You were there that day, weren't you? That's what's driven you so hard. They killed my parents and they tried to kill you, but you escaped. You know all about it, don't you? And you never told me."

Casski, still watching Ahmed, found her in his peripheral vision.

"All true, Sue. Now that this is winding down, I'll tell you everything I know. But not just yet. First we have to deal with Ahmed."

Peter had backed away from him, leaving the Sudanese spread-eagled against the wall. "He's clean," Peter said.

"Turn around," Casski said.

Ahmed turned, facing them.

Beside him Casski could hear Sue's breath coming in short, shallow gasps. She was staring at the man who killed her parents; he couldn't blame her for what she was feeling.

"We're going to send you back for debriefing," Casski said to Ahmed. "Don't hold any noble thoughts about not cooperating. You'll cooperate. In a few moments I'll call in the backup. They'll take you away and ask you some questions. And when they're through with you, Ahmed, I'm going to get them to put us in a room, alone."

Ahmed stared at Casski. "I would like that," he said in almost unaccented English. "I should have killed you quickly and simply, but I listened to Kopalev. He liked to kill in different ways."

"But he was just an assassin," Casski said, with heavy sarcasm, "while you are an instrument of Allah, and a sword of the revolution."

"You may scoff," Ahmed said quietly, "but we are winning. And we will continue and continue and continue until you are finished. We have what you call the staying power for this war; you do not."

"What makes you think so?" Casski asked.

"You are soft. Your men are pleasure oriented. Your women are whores. You have no beliefs, no religion. You are driven only by money and you seek gratification, not a better world. We will win because we are tougher than you, and because we believe in something.''

''You killed them for your beliefs?'' Sue said, almost in a whisper. ''You killed my parents because your beliefs were different? My God, don't you have any feelings at all?''

Ahmed watched her. Casski thought he saw something in the dark man's eyes.

''I have feelings,'' Ahmed said. ''I enjoyed watching them die. They died slowly and in agony. They died—''

Sue flung herself at him, in a frenzy.

She passed right in front of Casski's line of fire, and even as he went into a crouch, throwing the .38 up in front of him, he knew there was no chance of firing, knew that Ahmed had lied about her parents' deaths— which, though violent, were not prolonged—in order to goad her into her reaction. The next few minutes would be critical.

Casski saw Ahmed's feet shift. *Not a killing stance, a counterpunch, a defensive position.* From the corner of his eye he saw Ah Po stretch futilely to grab for Sue, saw Carlton shift farther to the right, a wrong move since it put him in jeopardy if there were a crossfire. As if it were slow motion, he saw Ahmed's body go into a slight crouch, the forearm block, the right leg rise in reflex, to block the kick that would follow if her attack was a feint. But it was not a feint; she just kept going in, driven by anger, going for his throat, his eyes, anything.

Casski saw Ahmed turn her as easily as if she were a child, sweeping her aside with the block, then following through in a graceful, turning motion that put her in front of him. He had one arm around her throat and with the other he twisted her right arm up her back, bending her backward in a cruel embrace. As he did it he pushed back against the wall, finding refuge in the wall behind him and the hostage in front.

"Son of a bitch," said Ah Po feelingly.

"Put the gun down, Casski," Ahmed said, no trace of emotion. "Put it down or I'll crush her windpipe."

There was a deadly stillness in the room.

"The last time, Casski. Put the gun on the floor. Bend down and place it to the left of you." Ahmed's voice was calm.

Casski leaned forward, put the gun down gently and straightened up again. Sue started to talk, but Ahmed merely flexed his arm, not more than a ripple of its strength, and Sue gasped for breath. "Now mine," Ahmed said. Casski took Ahmed's gun from his jacket pocket and put it down beside his own.

"You talk when I say talk," Ahmed said into Sue's ear.

Casski watched from the corner of his eye as Carlton's right hand slowly inched toward the inside of his jacket. Don't do it, he thought, don't let him see.... But he had seen.

"Take the weapon out slowly," Ahmed said to Carlton. "Put it on the floor. I can snap her windpipe faster than you can point and fire."

"Damn," said Ah Po, looking disgusted.

"Do as he says," Casski told Carlton.

Carlton slipped his hand out of the jacket, holding the gun by the handle, his finger well away from the trigger. From where Casski stood it looked like a Llama, probably the .32 that was so popular. Casski watched as he put it on the floor, wondering if he had pushed the safety off.

"Now," said Ahmed. "How many guards are there outside?"

"Four," Casski said.

"That means eight or six," Ahmed said. "Inside?"

"What difference does it make, if you won't believe me?" Casski said, his mind racing. There was an easy way to break the grip Ahmed had on her, if she'd had some training.

"Inside?" Ahmed asked again. Once more he moved his arm ever so slightly, and Casski heard Sue's breath go raspy.

"None," Casski replied. "We moved them all out when Mrs. Li let me in earlier."

"They must think a lot of you, Casski...and you must be a big disappointment to them."

"Kopalev and Wu aren't here to support that view," Casski said. Ahmed merely stared at him with his dead eyes.

"Turn her loose," Casski said, "and I'll go into the room alone with you, right now."

Ahmed spoke into Sue's ear, but so that all could hear him. "We're going out . . . out of this room and past the stairs, down the hallway and out the front door. We are going to walk slowly down the road to the gate. If a guard appears, I will kill you...so you, old woman, if you want her to live, you contain the guards."

Ah Po nodded. "I will," she said huskily.

"Casski, you and this one will walk ahead of me until we reach the door. There you will lie on the floor. First you will give me the weapons."

"No," said Casski.

"Then I will kill her here and now," Ahmed said, his voice still calm and unemotional.

"Do it, Casski," Carlton said. Casski glanced at him. There was an urgency in his eyes. "Do it, dammit, Casski."

"Slide the gun over," Ahmed said.

Casski felt cold. Buy time, and *think*!

"I can't slide the damn thing on this carpet," Casski said. "Got any other ideas?"

"Back away," said Ahmed.

Casski began to move slowly backward, feeling Ah Po also moving back, never taking her eyes off Ahmed and Sue. Carlton, off to the right, stood still.

Casski backed until he sensed something behind him, and shot a glance back and down. It was a small table with a dragon statue on it. Casski moved until he was touching the table.

Ahmed shuffled forward, forcing Sue in front of him. Carefully he inched toward Casski's gun, keeping a wary eye on Carlton as he moved. Suddenly he stopped.

"I don't like where you're standing," he said to Carlton. "Move the gun to the left side with your foot and then go to your right." He waited for Carlton.

Casski watched Carlton. The man seemed to be moving with a kind of detachment. And what was it he had seen in Carlton's eyes? *Do it*, he had urged. He tried to read Carlton's face, and incredibly, when Carlton moved closer into the center of events, Casski thought he saw a small smile on the handsome face.

He's up to something, Casski thought, feeling the hope springing back. But what? And how can I help? Instinctively, Casski pressed harder against the edge of the table. *Think!*

Ahmed started inching forward again. Casski watched Sue. In spite of the paleness of her face, she was composed. Her head was bent back at an unnatural angle, and her breath was coming in short gasps, but she was calm and beautiful and the glint in her eyes was one of anger, not fear. Casski was proud of her, and a lot of other feelings surged toward the surface. *Stop it! Think!*

And then he thought he knew what Carlton wanted.

Ahmed pushed her past Casski's gun. He began to crouch, forcing Sue down with him.

Ahmed reached for the gun.

Casski gave a violent push with his hips. The table rocked and the dragon statue plummeted heavily to the floor.

The crash was sudden and loud, and it came as Ahmed was picking up the gun. He threw Sue forward and closed his hand around Casski's .38, all in one easy motion, swinging the gun up and up, to center it on Casski's chest.

"Ahmed!"

Carlton's yell caused Ahmed to swing around. Casski saw him look at Carlton and hesitate, ever so briefly.

From somewhere Carlton had produced a second gun, and Casski had guessed right. The other man had needed a diversion.

Ahmed's split second of indecision was enough. Carlton fired once.

Casski saw the hole appear in the center of Ahmed's forehead, and in the sound of the blast, saw the blood and bone fly away from the back of his head, saw the head snap back and drag the body with it.

Ahmed was dead before his body hit the floor.

In the seconds that followed Casski was conscious of the smell of the gunpowder, of Sue turning on the floor and staring back at Ahmed, of the grandmother starting forward to comfort her.

Casski tore his gaze away and looked at Peter Carlton.

"Always carry a spare," the younger man said flippantly, and as he put the second gun away in his waistband, he favored Casski with a boyish and triumphant smile.

TEN

"YOU'VE ALL GOT Casski's briefing fixed in mind," Anderson said, not making it a question, daring any negative replies.

"Essentially," he said, "Casski's part in this is over. He's killed—or at least managed the deaths of—the three people who killed the Martins and damned near killed him. So I think at this point we can close the books on that aspect of the case."

He looked around the room. He was getting to know them so well now, their idiosyncrasies, their habits, their intellectualism or lack of it. He knew when to push their buttons, and when to back off.

And they knew him, too. He could tell by the way they watched him that they weren't satisfied. And he knew who would be the first to bring it up.

From behind a wreath of pipe smoke, Sinclair launched his gentlemanly Virginia drawl. "I can sense that you aren't all that thrilled at the outcome, Andy. You want to tell us what's bothering you?"

Anderson pulled on his earlobe. The others in the room waited.

"The Martins got killed," Anderson said at last, "because someone tipped the Jihad that we were an eyelash away from cranking up Longbow, and Martin certainly would have been a big part of it. I don't think anyone knew the Middle East like he did. It seemed obvious the *Jihadia* were trying to put a wrinkle in it even before Longbow began.''

"Now…we're a composite group. We leave this room and—except for me—all go back to our respective organizations. We use the assets of those various organizations, depending on what we need and when we need it. There's enormous opportunity for some sleeper or double, or some traitor burning with revolutionary zeal—hell, even some money-hungry clerk—to blow our operations. Since our operations are counterterrorism, our primary targets have been the assassins of the Jihad, and the governments that support terrorism.''

Anderson paused. "I don't mean to overkill with the lecture," he said. "I just want to make sure you understand what's happened here.''

Sinclair nodded and Anderson went on.

"Our aims happened to coincide with Casski's, who used to work for me. I had him on the Martins because we had the foresight to know that Martin could be a target. Hindsight tells us that we should have paid much more attention to them, and that Casski couldn't be everywhere at once. The operation the terrorists mounted could only have been stopped by a small navy.

"So they sent out their best thugs and got the Martins. Miracle of miracles, Casski survived, and because he's the type that demands revenge, we turned him loose on the three killers. Happily, he's done them in, as you know.

"Along the way we began to see a pattern emerging. Many of our operations were being countered. We set up some dummy ones and they would have been blown, had we gone through with them. I put the computer boys working on a little theory that we had a snake in the barn, and by God, we did.

"This was a long answer, but I wanted to make it clear. The reason I'm unhappy is that the goddamned snake is still alive and well, somewhere. We've knocked over the three assassins that got Martin, but we haven't got the bastard that ordered it."

Akers cleared his throat.

"Yes, Admiral?" Anderson said wearily.

"What moves have we made toward finding the snake?"

"Ahmed killed our best computer expert, and we've had to start over. If you'll remember, I told you that the snake isn't one of us in this room. That took a lot of mathematics, matching the odds with the events. We're assuming it is a senior field man, as I also told you earlier."

Anderson leaned forward. "What I've told Casski is that the traitor is also a fourth assassin—the one who ordered the Martin killings, the one who's done some other wet operations on his own."

"Is it true?" Sinclair asked.

"I don't know," Anderson admitted. "But it's one way of keeping Casski with us as long as possible. I sure like having him on our side."

Anderson let the silence spread.

"What's the next move?" Akers asked.

"Got to keep all the computer boys on overtime," Anderson replied. "Before he left here for his Hawaii vacation and got killed, Campbell told me it was a matter of applied mathematics. We just keep plugging away until something in someone's dossier matches an equation for being in enough right places at the right times. At some point," Anderson said, his voice lowering, "at some point, we're going to be able to put a name and a face onto someone who's been in a position to cause all this damage. I think we can do it soon."

"And then what?" asked Sinclair.

"God help him," said Anderson.

AH PO LOOKED OUT through the gauze drapery to where her granddaughter stood on the veranda. All of Hong Kong was spread out before the girl—she could see over into Kowloon and beyond, up toward the New Territories and the border, over toward the islands. She could look down on the gleaming white towers of commerce, on the teeming junks, on the rust-bucket freighters in the harbor, and at the U.S. destroyer, a part of the Seventh Fleet. It was a day of high cumulus clouds and a sea that threw back diamonds in the calm of the morning.

She isn't seeing any of it, Ah Po thought.

Damn Casski.

In the aftermath of that terrible night, Ah Po had been sure that Sue and Casski would, at last, be able to reconcile something. They were so much in love it hurt just to watch them...so what was the problem? Ah Po thought she knew: Sue looked at Casski and saw more than a man she loved; she saw a link to her parents. She might forever worry about Casski leaving her, or dying, rejecting her in some way. But, Ah Po thought, she would be willing to try. The fault lay with Casski, an old curmudgeon if ever she'd seen one. He just didn't want to give up his independence. He loved Sue, but perhaps he carried a slight sense of guilt, too. He had been unable to stop the assassins from killing her parents. In all likelihood, it couldn't have been stopped. Casski was only one man, and Ah Po knew her son-in-law; he wasn't the type to stay undercover forever, and a sailboat was obviously a terribly vulnerable place to be.

Then there was the fact that Casski felt protective, almost fatherly. It was the quickest way to kill romance, becoming a familiar part of the family. Still, from the look on Casski's face that night, what he felt now was far from fatherly. That terrible assassin hadn't been dead thirty seconds before Casski had swept Sue up and was holding her, stroking her hair and letting her cry into his chest. It was the other one, Peter, the good-looking one, who finally called someone, and a whole team of specialists arrived to take over.

They had moved the body out immediately—it was a mess. The guards, the ones Casski had instructed to let Ahmed infiltrate unless he tried to kill them, had helped clean things up and then moved off. (The next day a small Chinese man had come to the house, bowed himself in and taken measurements. The dragon room had been refurnished with new carpeting, new wallpaper and new upholstery.) Then Casski had gotten into a long conversation with the leader of the specialists. Finally, near dawn, they had been able to sit down—Casski, Peter, Sue and herself—and enjoy a well-deserved drink. Sue was drawn but poised, and her eyes never left Casski's face. Sometimes Ah Po would catch him looking back, his eyes and face revealing more than she had seen before—more, she was sure, than he wanted everyone to see.

Ah Po walked out onto the veranda and stood beside her granddaughter. "Beloved child," she said gently, "how would you like to go over to Happy Valley and bet a little on the horses?"

Sue's smile was wistful. "I don't think so, Ah Po. Thank you for asking."

"All right," Ah Po persisted, "how about taking the hydrofoil with me to Macau, and we'll play some mah-jongg?"

Sue shook her head.

Ah Po reached out and took her hand. "You will see him again, my dear. The silly bastard has got to go away and work it out for himself. But it will happen. Trust me."

Sue turned and put her arms around her grandmother. "You're wonderful, Ah Po."

"Damned right," Ah Po said. "But for right now, let's make some plans, hey? Come have some tea, or a drink. I can feel you're getting ready to go on again, so let's talk about it. Never try to hide anything from your old grandmother."

CASSKI PAUSED in front of the kitchen counter. Dinner was simmering, the Jamieson's was within reach, and there was plenty of strong black coffee. He went out on the porch of the cabin and looked down the road. Nothing yet. Back inside, he pushed six rounds into the Winchester .30-30 and put it carefully on the pegs of the beam that divided the cabin's living room and kitchen areas. Then, considering, he reached up and took down the Winchester, chambered a round and cocked it before putting it up again, very carefully. One of the first things he had learned is that a gun not ready for action becomes a hell of a liability.

He had planned to allow himself one good shot of Jamieson's, and he decided to have it now. He drank it neat, standing on the porch and watching the sun dancing, and hearing the silence. He had been back only a week, and already it felt good. But it felt lonely, too. It was a feeling so strange, so foreign to him, that he had had trouble identifying it at first. And when he did he had tried to deny it, then ignore it, and finally come to grips with it. He shook his head. Time for that later.

He was wearing an old flannel shirt and jeans, boots and a worn leather belt with a knife in it. He felt good, strong, elemental, a part of this scene. Yet . . . he knew now he could leave it if he had to. He could stay, or he could go, where once he could only stay. He walked around and looked at the stack of wood, looked beyond the utility shed at the land stretching away in all directions.

She had told him about her cabin, in a rush of words just before he left Hong Kong. It's there, she said. It's always been there for me, so I think that's where I'm going now. She had left the next part open. I have to go to Washington, he said, knowing he was just filling in the silence. Then I'll go out to the ranch in Idaho. I want to think, Sue. Yes, she had said, but let me tell you about the cabin. And so she had. He liked to think about her in her little A-frame, in normal circumstances, the way she described it. Not too far away, actually. He could be there in two hours: flight time and a drive.

And once again, as he had for the hundredth time that day, he remembered who else knew about it.

He walked back toward his cabin, and heard the telephone ringing.

He went inside and picked up the receiver. "Hello."

"One of them is coming," said the voice, an old, husky voice, the kind of voice a man has when he is not used to talking that much. Casski smiled to think of the old Indian standing at a telephone. Nothing invented by the whites could ever please the old Shoshone, except a good rifle.

"Which one is it?" Casski said, afraid of the answer.

"The one with the circle on the back of the picture, like the moon."

Casski's heart sank. "All right," he said. "How long ago?"

"Not much." That would be within the past half hour.

"Come yourself then," he said to the old Shoshone. "You know the place. There'll be enough food and whisky for a week. I'll be back in a week. If I'm not, the place is yours."

He heard the Indian grunt. "Maybe I kill you myself."

"I telephoned Ah Po. She was going one of two places—there, or here."

"Ah," said Anderson. "It's falling into place. A cri de coeur answered by the knight, rescuing the maiden in the castle, an affair of the heart . . ."

"Knock off the shit, Andy, and finish your stew. We haven't got a hell of a lot of time."

"I could put men on it," Anderson said, pulling his earlobe. "Western regional office could have a team in there."

"I can see it now," Casski said nastily, "thugs going in accompanied by the public relations division. They'd do everything but take out an ad, and they'd get her killed for sure. No, this is mine, and I'm going to finish it."

"What can I do to help, then?" Anderson asked.

"Drive me to an airport. Talk to me on the way. Use your influence to get me on the plane carrying the .38, and maybe the Winchester, wrapped up. Give me a little time. Then, and only then, you can send in the Marines."

"Ready when you are."

Casski scraped the dishes and put them in the sink, then got down the Winchester and wrapped it in an old oilskin, trying to disguise the shape. He picked up a fleece-lined jacket, turned out the light and followed Anderson out onto the porch. The darkness had settled in and the stars were glinting in a clear sky. "Nice here," Anderson said, and "Yeah, let's go," Casski replied.

The car made a U-turn and hurtled away. Casski sat back and closed his eyes, trying to empty his mind. Unsuccessfully.

Finally he glanced at Anderson. "What have we learned from all this?" he asked.

"Strange question, coming from you."

"What I mean is, aside from the operational aspects of trying to stop those mindless bastards, what are we learning about how to get at the cause of all this?"

"You want the quickie course?"

"It's all we've time for."

"There are two types of terrorists," Anderson said. "There's the bunch that want a homeland, Palestinians who want to settle down on their own land. They want to pressure the U.S. and Israel into giving them what they want. Then there's the Islamic militants; they want to annihilate anybody who seems to be threatening their way of life, and their religion. It's this latter group that inspired the Jihad . . . and it's the Jihad that hired Kopalev and Ahmed and Wu...and in time, others. Within those two broad categories are dozens of factions, sometimes at each other's throats. The big danger for the U.S. is that one day these assholes will settle down and patch up their differences and present a solid front. That's the point where we'll see terrorism elevated to new and dangerous heights."

"A solution?"

"Well . . . we like to think Longbow is one solution. An American public aware of the potential problems is a help toward finding solutions. Getting the Arabs and the Israelis to a conference table would help."

Casski could see Anderson hesitating. "And?"

"And...we could defuse the militants, eliminate some of the tensions, make a few concessions. I know that sounds un-American, but we can't forever equate foreign policy with our ability to retaliate militarily. Whatever solution we find, for it to be permanent, it will have to be accomplished through statecraft."

"By the time you do that," Casski said meanly, "there's going to be one less terrorist. You can bet on that."

"Can't say I blame you, Cass." Anderson kept the pressure on the accelerator as the car drove through the quiet night.

IT WAS A FINE OPERA and a recording of great fidelity, but Sue listened impatiently until it reached the aria that she considered the finest ever written. Cio-cio-san began the lyrical and poignant "Un Bel Di," and Sue abandoned herself to the passion and power of the aria, standing at the high window and looking out, unseeing, to where the trees marched down and then up again, to the ridge that itself rose to join the mountains.

She let the notes pour around her, filling the cabin and rising to the apex of the A-frame, notes that tumbled and soared and echoed the wash of emotions in her own heart.

This is what love is, a knowledge that sometimes comes too late. Or a knowledge that has no margin for error. But she had tried. She had warned Casski that what she was feeling was deeper than he knew; she had tried to draw him out. From the depths of that failure she had turned, however briefly, however unwillingly, to the attentions of another. Thank God there had been nothing serious with Peter, no matter how charming he was. At one time she had felt he was exactly what she needed—a boyish, carefree, happy soul who could make her laugh, who could joke his way out of depression and take her with him. *He is a charming boy, but Casski is a man.* Casski didn't lack charm, in his own way; he just never bothered to use it when he didn't have to.

Madame Butterfly sang of love and loss. Sue felt no sense of loss. She would find Casski one day, when they both felt it, when the miles apart became too far, the time too long. One fine day they would meet again.

She switched off the record and stood watching the play of sunlight on the ridge, the deep shadows of the small coves, seeing the wind causing a slight bend in the tops of the trees. She had been in the cabin for several days, enjoying the solitude, enjoying the time to think.

She had buried a lot of ghosts recently, and she felt that the spirits of her parents were resting at last. It had begun here in the cabin, with the telephone call that had told her of her parents' murder. So much had happened since, so many miles. And it had all ended in Ah Po's house. Fitting, somehow.

Outside, she thought. Time to get out and walk.

She was wearing jeans and running shoes and an old gray sweatshirt. Over it she pulled a blue jacket. In the refrigerator she found a couple of granola bars and stuffed them in the jacket pocket. She took the keys from the rung by the door and stepped out, locking the door behind her.

The day was clear and cool, but not cold, with a slight breeze from the northwest. In the distance she could see the lake shimmering, glinting like metal in the strong sun. She felt the ground crunch underfoot, felt the strength and youth of her body. When she entered the tree line the shadows and sunlight dropped over her like a striped cape, changing constantly but somehow the same. The pine needles were soft to walk on, and the air was suddenly scented.

She walked for fifteen minutes or so and came out of the trees again, higher now, well up on the side of the ridge. She walked parallel to the ridge line, facing the sun and feeling its warmth even through the coolness. It was a glorious day, and she was smiling.

She sensed, rather than heard the car.

She turned and at once saw it, stopping by the cabin. A figure got out, partially hidden by the car. She held her breath, her heart racing. Then the figure came from behind the car, and it was not the blocky silhouette she would have known anywhere.

But it was familiar.

"Peter," she called. "Up here." She yelled and waved.

She saw him look around, then walk up to the cabin. He must have tried the door, she thought, because he was back by the car in a moment. The car door opened and closed again, and he stood beside it, shading his eyes. Then she caught the glint of glass and knew he was using binoculars. She grinned and waved, and all at once he waved back, an exuberant and joyful wave. She saw him open the car door again, obviously putting away the binoculars, then slam it. He started toward her, jogging easily. She watched until he entered the tree line.

She found a small outcropping and sat down, waiting happily. *All right, it isn't Casski, but it's a friend, and after all, you told him one time how to get here, so be the gracious hostess. Besides, you know he'll make you laugh. And admit it: once you were more than friends, you were lovers. Your first love.*

She watched him emerge from the trees and start up, the hardest part of the climb. He took it easily, gracefully, and she could see him grinning as he switched back and forth, skirting the rocks and working above the timberline until he was on the same ridge as she was, level with her and approaching at a trot.

"You must be in great shape, Peter Carlton," she called.

He stopped. "And I've always admired yours," he yelled back, then came on at a ground-eating pace.

She stood up as he approached. "That's sinful," she said. "You aren't even breathing hard."

"Hello, Sue," he said, and swept her up in a hug. He held her for a moment and then kissed her lightly on the lips, a kiss of total friendship, not at all sensual.

"Sit with me," she said. "The view's terrific. Have a granola bar. How do you like my countryside? What do you think of the cabin? Isn't it all I said it was?"

He considered. "Okay. Yes. I will. It's fantastic. It's smaller than I thought, and yes, it is." He grinned.

"You're still crazy," she said, and handed him one of the bars.

They ate in companionable silence. After a time he said, "It's incomparable. You're lucky to have this."

"I know," she said. "And lucky to have you as my good friend, Peter."

When he didn't reply she turned her head. He was staring at her.

"I heard the sound of that," he said finally. "Shoot, I'm always going to have you as a friend? I had hopes for more." But he smiled gently, taking the sting out of the words.

"Peter," she said. "You know, don't you?"

He nodded. "Yeah, I know. It's that damned Casski."

"Not 'damned' Casski," she protested, laughing.

"Does he know what he's got?"

Sue paused. "I think so. I think he's just been fighting it."

"The way he looked at you that night . . . you know, the night Ahmed came. It told me a lot."

"Hey, Peter," she said, "I learned some things, too. Like who employs you."

"What?" he said.

"Longbow. Casski's people. I didn't know until that night you were one of them."

"Are you disappointed?"

"Don't be silly. Just surprised. You always seemed too happy-go-lucky for that kind of work."

"Great cover," he said.

"That night in Bangkok, onstage. You were right on top of things. I should have known then." When he didn't reply she turned to face him again. "What is it?" she asked.

"I thought I heard something," he said quietly. He was standing now, taut as a bowstring, looking down into the trees below.

"Probably a deer, or an elk," she said. "Lots of them here."

"Sounded like an engine."

"Do you see another car?"

"No. Sure sounded like an engine, though."

"It could have been anything. Even the occasional rock slide up here sounds like the end of the world."

She looked for the reassuring grin, and was surprised to find him very still and unsmiling. "What's the matter, Peter?"

"Sue, listen..." he began, and something in his voice caused her to glance up at him. He was looking at her with an expression she couldn't read. "You know...I've always loved you."

"Even when I was just an assignment?" She said it without bitterness.

"You were much more. Much more. But now..."

She waited, but he was silent. She drew away from him a little. "What is it, Peter?"

Still he was silent, facing away from her.

"Peter, my dear, for all we've been to each other, what *is* it?"

She waited.

And heard Casski's voice. "He's trying to tell you that he came here to kill you."

They spun around. Casski stood there, holding a rifle in his right hand, nestling it in the crook of his left arm and standing sideways. His stance was relaxed and easy, his voice calm.

"Back away from him, Sue."

She was staring at Peter, her face frozen in shock.

"Peter," she said. It was hardly more than a whisper.

"His code name is Scimitar," Casski said. "The fourth man."

Her eyes swept the handsome boyish face. She turned to Casski. "Tell me," she said.

"I will," Casski said. He hadn't moved. "But first get farther away from him. Come over here, by me, to the left and back of me a little."

When she had moved Casski shifted slightly, never moving the Winchester.

"This one—" he nodded at the assassin "—was assigned to you in Hong Kong. Through you he would get inside the Martin household, find out what your father was up to, see what he knew. It just didn't work out, and your father moved too fast, getting you out of town and into deep cover. Scimitar—I don't know his real name—finally just ordered your parents' death. He would have killed you, too, if you'd been around, just on the off chance you knew something."

"I understand that," Sue said, her eyes still on Peter. "But he could have killed me since. Many times."

"Stringing you along," Casski said. "Trying to see what else he could learn. And he was getting close to you as a way of getting close to me. As you said in Tahiti, you were the bait."

"You mean..."

"When the others failed, he decided to go ahead with it, and kill us both. After you he would have come for me."

Scimitar moved his feet, ever so slightly.

"Reach in and get the gun by the butt and toss it behind you," Casski said. "If I see your finger move I'll kill you."

"You'd like to kill me anyway," Scimitar said.

"You want to test that theory?" Casski asked.

Scimitar's hand went into his jacket and came back with the gun, held very carefully. He tossed it behind him.

"Now the other one," Casski said. "You always carry a spare, remember?"

With his left hand Scimitar reached into his waistband beneath his jacket and eased out the small automatic. He flipped it underhand, behind him.

"That night in Bangkok..." Sue began.

"He fired the shot himself, jumped into the situation to help establish his credibility with you... and, I suppose, with me. You see, it was some time before Anderson told me that this bastard was one of us—at least he was *supposed* to be one of us."

She stared with loathing at the man she had known as Peter Carlton. He had held her, kissed her, made love to her. She could remember his hands on her. She could remember the bitter fights she had had with her parents about him, convinced he was the reason she was being sent away. The irony was they *had* sent her away because of him—for her own safety. He had held her, this man, then had gone out and ordered her parents killed.

Casski sensed the shift in her mood. "I know how you feel," he said. "I'm pissed because it took so long to find him."

Scimitar cleared his throat and waited. Casski felt a slight change in the wind direction.

"How did you find him?" Sue asked finally.

"Anderson had his computers running. He finally doped it out that the fourth man was able to make the others so effective because he was on the inside of the antiterrorist activities. Anderson matched hypothetical events and the profiles in our dossiers. When it became clear that some positive connections could be made, he pulled the hypothetical stuff and fed the computers actual data. That's when Ahmed killed his top computer man, Campbell, in Hawaii. But he kept going with it, and the computers narrowed it down to a couple of equations. Carlton was one of them. We matched what we knew about Scimitar from other sources, mostly Israeli, and we got a number of possibilities that finally narrowed down to Carlton once again."

Scimitar suddenly grinned. "You beat the computers, though, didn't you, Casski? Must have given you some real satisfaction. Your dossier noted that you hate gadgets."

"How?" asked Sue.

"In Hong Kong, the night we set an ambush for Ahmed. Scimitar decided to kill him if it looked like Ahmed might be captured. Ahmed might have gotten out alive, but then he might not have. So he shot him."

"What made you sure?" Scimitar asked.

Casski smiled thinly. "Ahmed waited ever so slightly after he swung the gun on you. I thought then it was stupid; I kept wondering why. He hesitated and you shot him. I ran through every reason I could think of for Ahmed to hesitate, and it finally came down to one."

"And here we are," said Scimitar.

"Yes."

"Now what, Casski? You plan to shoot me here? Anderson wouldn't like that."

"I know," said Casski.

Sue moved up a little to stand beside Casski. Holding the Winchester steady in his right hand, he pushed her back gently with his left.

"Anderson wants to bring him back?" she asked.

"Yes. For what he knows."

Her eyes searched Casski's face. "Well?"

"There's another angle to this," Casski said. "He's made me mad."

Scimitar laughed, a carefree, infectious laugh. "Don't be stupid, Casski. You won't kill me. You're under orders, like all the others. You'll take me back to Anderson. I'll be locked up, at least for a while, and I'll tell them everything they want to know about the Jihad. I'll bargain for my life and I'll get it, Casski."

"What makes you so sure?" Casski asked.

"Because you're all soft, as Ahmed used to tell me at length. It's the upbringing and the training, the stupid morality, the American sense of fair play. In the end you won't shoot me because I'm unarmed. I'm your pris-

oner. So let's quit screwing around and get on with it.
I'm tired of standing here.''

"Me too," said Casski, and squeezed the trigger.

The shot tore through Scimitar's heart, hurling him backward. He landed on his back with his head down-hill, his shirt and jacket already blood-soaked, his eyes open and staring.

Casski turned to Sue. "Martin Tsu-wei," he said, "walk down the hill and wait for me in the trees."

She stood, staring at Scimitar's body. The blood had drained from her face. Casski walked over and shook her gently but she stood there, rooted. He slapped her.

Her head jerked up.

"Walk down the hill," he said. "Wait for me in the trees."

Without a word she turned and went down.

When he saw her disappear into the trees he turned back to the assassin. He put the barrel of the Winchester behind Scimitar's ear. He worked the lever-action and put another round in the chamber. Then he shot him again, just to be sure.

He turned and went down into the trees.

She was standing just inside the tree line, shaking like a leaf.

"You killed him," she said, her voice flat.

"Damned right I did," Casski said. "It felt good, too."

They looked at each other for a long moment.

"Come on," Casski said, and took her hand. He led her out of the trees and back to the cabin, where she stood, staring fixedly at the door.

"Give me the keys."

Mechanically she handed him the keys and he unlocked the door. He led her inside, taking in the cabin at a glance. He pushed her gently onto a couch and went to the fireplace. After he poked at the logs the flames began to catch again. He searched until he found the liquor and poured each of them a brandy. He had to unbend her fingers to get her to hold it, and when he looked back at her she hadn't touched it. He sat across from her on a chair and sipped the brandy and waited. After a while she began to drink, slowly.

They heard the cars at the same time.

"That'll be Anderson's people," he said. "You can wait here." He went outside.

She heard voices, and one of them sounded angry. After a while she heard them move off.

They're going to get Peter's body, she thought. She began to shake again.

Casski came back into the cabin. "Listen to me," he said.

But she was afraid to. She put her head in her hands.

He sat down beside her and she felt his strong arms around her. "Listen to me," he said again. And he began to talk.

He told her everything he knew. He told her about the terrible day on the yacht in Repulse Bay, about the gunfire and the flames, about the death of her parents and his own miraculous escape. He filled her in on all the events since, the things she couldn't have known, the search for the traitor in Longbow. Once he got up to poke at the wood in the fireplace, sending a shower of sparks up the chimney. After a while she noticed it was dark outside, the room lit only by the firelight. And in time, when he had told it all, he stopped.

"Come," he said.

He led her into the bathroom and undressed her, and himself. She felt nothing at all. He took her into the shower and ran the water over them, and soaped her and himself thoroughly, and when they were clean he did it all again, holding her gently in the cleansing water.

When he had dried them both he led her up to the sleeping loft and turned down the comforter on the bed. There was a dim light coming from the fireplace. He helped her into bed and got in beside her and lay next to her in the dark, not touching. After a long time he heard her regular breathing and knew she was asleep.

When he opened his eyes again there was daylight in the room and she was awake, watching him. He reached for her and she moved into his arms, and began to cry.

He let her cry, until she finally stopped and turned away from him and went into the bathroom. He waited.

"I look awful," she said, and he began to grin.

She came back out. "What are you laughing at, you big ape?"

"I think you're back to normal."

She stood looking down at him. "It's over, isn't it?" she said.

"Well and truly over," he replied.

She sat on the edge of the bed, suddenly aware of her nakedness, a little shy.

"Now what?" she asked, not looking at him.

"Christ, woman, what about some breakfast?"

She turned suddenly and headed for the ladder down to the main floor of the cabin. He watched her go, grinning to himself. She made a great exit.

A few minutes later he heard the first notes of a symphony. Brahms, he thought. The music rose in all its richness and glory, melodic and grand. She came back up the ladder and over to the bed.

She reached down and threw back the comforter and got back into bed with him. "Breakfast comes later," she said.

EPILOGUE

THE OLD FISHERMAN squatted near the black rocks, his conical hat low on his forehead. He squinted out to the bay where the waters were blue and green, darkened by the coral heads underneath. He could see the isolated ripples where the wind was gusting slightly on the surface of the water.

A junk came into the bay, rounding the headland easily under sail. It moved quickly toward the beach, then the sails dropped suddenly. The fisherman heard the splash of anchors. As he watched, a boat pushed off from the junk; besides the pair at the oars, it carried a man, a woman and an assortment of boxes.

The boat came up to the beach, not far from where the old fisherman sat. He saw the doctor-priest, Lin, walk down to the beach. The man and woman got out of the boat, splashing in the water. He could hear the woman's laugh. She was young, he saw, and beautiful. He thought she might have Chinese blood.

The man with her was large and tough-looking. The old fisherman knew him instantly, for not many *kwai-lohs* came to the island. He was the man washed in by the surf, the badly burned man whom the priests brought back to health. Now the *kwai-loh* stood, one arm around the girl, and with the other he was shaking hands with Lin. The old fisherman could hear them talking loud and quickly, and laughing.

After a time they all helped unload the boxes. They were of various sizes and shapes, but all had red crosses painted on them, like the boxes with the *kwai-loh* medicines the priests kept. The two oarsmen helped carry the boxes, and the procession moved out of the fisherman's vision, heading inland.

The fishing was slow, but he was in no hurry, and several hours passed.

He had put new bait on his hook when he heard them come out of the bush again, and into his view. The *kwai-loh* and the girl stopped while the two oarsmen got the boat into position. The *kwai-loh* and Lin shook hands, and the girl took both of Lin's hands in hers. She said something that made the doctor-priest laugh. Then they got back into the boat, leaving Lin standing on the sand.

When the boat reached the junk, they clambered aboard. The boat was secured at the stern, to trail behind, and the junk hauled anchors aboard. A moment later the lateen sails went up and the junk swung to starboard. As it began to move out of the little bay, the old fisherman could see figures on board, waving, and on the beach Lin waved in answer. The junk left the bay and caught the off-shore swells, and then it rounded the headland and was gone.

The old fisherman shifted slightly, careful to keep his shadow out of the water eddying around the rocks. He looked toward the horizon. The wind had picked up and there were a few whitecaps. The sun had moved to his right, as it always did this time of year, when he fished by these rocks. It was a strong sun for the season, and it threw a bright yellow light over the island and the sea.

From the bestselling author of *Air Glow Red* and *Storm*, a state-of-the-art suspense two thousand feet below the waves.

DEEP CHILL

IAN SLATER

When an eighteen-thousand-ton nuclear submarine sinks in the icy North Pacific on the U.S.-Soviet border, a dying crew are trapped inside with Pentagon's most vital secrets. Oceanographer Frank Hall accepts an impossible mission as he descends into the silent depths and becomes caught in a life-threatening race with the Soviets.